The Insidious Line

tales from the archetypes:

Volume 3

'The Superior'

By

Paul Ogden

'For no matter how close you believe you are to the truth
You will never be near enough.'

Dedicated to the Truth Seekers
And all those who work in Love

Table of Contents

Preface   1

Part 1 – The Line of the Path   2

Chapter 1: The Chairman   8
Chapter 2: The Aunt   31

Part 2 – The Chiming of the Bell   46

Chapter 3: The Victim   49
Chapter 4: The Lady with the bag   61
Chapter 5: The Pastor (who was retired)   82
Chapter 6: The Politician   105

Part 3 – The Journey towards Truth   133

Chapter 7: The Chief Executive   137
Chapter 8: The Evangelist   155
Chapter 9: The Guru   172

Conclusion   198

Chapter 10: The Child   200

Acknowledgements   202
About the Author   203

Preface

'Listen only for the truth which seeks not to limit your imagination.'

The early morning bell rings out across the Ashram calling for the start of a new day. The old man awakes - he has been dreaming about her again. He barely acknowledges the chimes as he registers the ache in his bones - in particular the hips.

He looks through the window before moving his dextral leg to the right in preparation for arising himself from the single bed. The response to this gentlest of manoeuvres is generated as an electrical stimulus through the peripheral nervous system, through the spine and into the thalamus, which then processes and relays the associated signals to the soma sensory cortex, the frontal cortex, and the limbic system. In the limited experience of human time all these signals appear to cognitively arrive at once resulting in his inevitable reaction - OUCH!

The old man moves his leg back into a comfortable position, groans and with a degree more thoughtfulness raises himself slowly out of the bed. He stands in front of the window for a moment looking out over the garden before moving carefully toward his bathroom. As he settles down for his toilette he sighs once more.

The old man has been waiting a long time for the guest to arrive - in fact he has been awaiting his arrival for many years now. He is tired and has lived within the proximity of the bell for too long - from the echo of its deepening chimes he is more than aware it is time to open the door.

Part 1 - The Line of the Path

'It is only in a moment when the Truth is revealed
If you were to look around what would you see?'

There is a path - a gift of destiny upon which you may wander. Within this benefaction there is also a choice - whether or not to travel consciously along the line on which your path has been directed or to ignore its very existence. When you were born your being was instinctively programmed to set out on this journey and seek the truth of what life had to offer you.

Everyone was granted this one gift, for, contrary to what some people would like you to believe, all individuals are born equal within the creation of their being. Nevertheless, this beneficence is hidden beyond ordinary everyday consciousness so there will be many who inevitably lose the intuitive ability they were bestowed with to follow the path, to find it, or to sense the very purpose of its existence. Consequently the line it follows is shrouded in a mist of ambiguity and countless numbers of your compatriots will deprive themselves of a vocation which was their birthright. For whilst everyone has been granted a destiny very few will actually achieve it.

And yet, regardless of this, each and everyone of you remains covenanted to a particular line of direction, and, for each and everyone of you, the path of destiny is uniquely different. If you are no longer following the line you will find yourself troubled - in reality suffering from a lack of direction. If this is the case there is nothing to fear for it is within the capacity of every living person to return - to continue consciously to follow the path and the line of its direction.

Can you see it? Can you feel it?

Our Universal Mother, Eve, discovered where the path of her destiny was leading after she had partaken of the delectable fruits propagated upon the tree of knowledge planted within the central courtyard of the Garden of Eden. She understood exactly that the line of its direction was leading towards the Source of Unknowable Truth. The knowledge she had imbibed from the unquenchable spirit of the fruits led her to instinctively realise the Choice; she could either follow the path to its ultimate destination, or disregard its very existence, remain still in one place and fall into the dream of forgetfulness.

Our Universal Mother lived a long and bountiful life, yet regardless of consciously suffering and willingly accepting the burden of destiny allotted upon her for climbing the tree and eating of the forbidden fruits, she was unable to realise the actualisation of this Truth before her death.

So here we are once again - the archetypes of your collective consciousness - to affect you with our presence, and, for one more time, assist you in the determination and revelation of your own personal truth and the possibilities concerning your future existence within the cycle of this current life.

We are your friends, fellow travellers and confidantes. Some of you have met us before and some of you will have forgotten we even exist. This is only natural within the overall limitations of your being and of course the relationship between us is complicated - for it is from you and your fellow travellers on this planet that we have imbibed within us the strength of our being.

As you may recall we are merely the embodiment of all human experience - the record of every action you undertake during the habitual routine of your daily life. Therefore, whilst we do not know exactly what the future will hold for you (as you have not yet lived it), we can predict the line of your direction with a certain degree of accuracy, because the behaviours of your past are the best predictors of your future.

But before we continue with our tales let us indulge the shortest moment of your time to reflect a little further concerning our understanding of human destiny.

It would appear that as soon as you are born you instinctively begin make your way forward on your own personal journey along the line of your path - how far you will travel, and whether you successfully reach the end, will be determined by whether or not you gain the ability to undertake the journey consciously. In the absence of such knowledge and understanding most of humanity follow the line passively, unwittingly straying from one side to another, stopping still, crossing it, and never realising where the dissatisfaction in their life originates from.

Yet to walk the line of your life consciously can be a painful preoccupation, especially when you come to realise how often you habitually move from one side of the path to the other without moving in any direction at all. And, more often than not, you may find yourself straying from the path and losing your way altogether - for the line it takes is insidious. Many who choose to follow their path consciously lose the way and in frustration give up the challenge - for to follow the line of your destiny faithfully without succumbing to sleep is virtually impossible.

Whilst it may seem unfair that the majority of your species become unaware of the path and the direction they should follow, especially as many will cross the line without realising the sin they have committed, it is, in fact, their choice to ignore the reality of their existence and sleep within the bliss of their own ignorance. For as we have already stated everyone born into your world is given the opportunity to be aware.

Yet collectively your species continually feel the need to create social structures and economic systems which encourage each and everyone living within their vicinity to fall asleep. These so called civilised societies promote an ideal way to live a life in order to contain, restrict and control the behaviour of its members. Living in the ideal way promoted by whatever ruling executive has attained domination is rewarded, and personal success within the culture is measured by its proletariat through the number of rewards an individual has managed to accumulate during their lifetime. What these rewards consist of differ from one culture to another but generally involve public recognition, wealth, and power over others less fortunate than themselves.

Many are swept along by the waves of collective hysteria in an endeavour to reap the temporal rewards on offer for adhering to the legislated controls placed upon their existence. As a consequence sleep is inevitable and the individual's ability to see the world as it is truly and most magnificently manifested is lost within whatever illusory craze has been mandated by their compatriots for their own mythical advancement.

Every social and economic structure is diametrically opposed to any other which disagrees with its own fundamental tenets regarding how life should be lived. Consequently each society will consider itself superior to any other existing within the same dimension of time. This simple fact is the apparent cause of all wars, the curse of which ensures the collapse of each and every civilisation throughout the many aeons of human existence.

Whilst this is obviously regrettable, we have to conclude it is the norm. People from opposing societies will continue to collectively kill one another regardless of the instinctive seed of conscience contained within each individual that this is an abhorrently wrong endeavour to engage with. And so civilisations will arise and fade away to be forgotten by each new generation emerging within their own truth.

The conundrum remains – the path of destiny for each civilisation is inevitable destruction and yet life as it is now lived cannot be sustained without a society to contain it.

However, an individual's path and the line it takes is quite separate from the culture within which they dwell, for no society can satisfy the innermost longing hidden within the depths of each human soul. Nor can any society know of or reveal the truth of the unique path each individual was gifted at birth.

During their life many people will hear tell of the path. Some will actively seek it out without realising the reality they are already travelling upon it.

The complexity for the uninitiated seeker is whilst they may rediscover their relationship with the path, they are unable to fathom where they are in relation to it or the line it takes - they know not whether they are moving forward or backwards, or whether they are moving left to right from one side or another.

All movement is subjected to the laws of cause and effect from which there is no escaping. The direction of each step is dependent on the previous step taken. All actions have a consequence and whether or not this has a positive or negative impact depends on the conscious intention of the traveller - for without conscious intention movement in any direction is random and the effect is unknown.

Your personal truth is found within the way you follow the line and the line itself is in constant movement under the controlling influence of the vine.

Naturally there are many individuals and organised religions who would claim to know all and everything about the path and the line of direction which should be taken along it. They will meander intentionally from one side and another claiming to be doing so on your behalf, waiting to initiate and bless you on your own personal journey. Beware of such people, especially if they seek any form of recompense for their labours, for it is generally their journey and not your own they wish to initiate upon you.

But for now, let us now continue with our tales - for there are some narratives we began to share with you previously which need finally to reach their conclusion. All accounts need to be settled before a journey can truly come to an end and we would like to share them with you as you continue upon your own journey within the space of time you have been allotted.

We are aware many of you have seen yourselves reflected within our words but let us assure you none of our stories are directly about you and your life. Of course there may be similarities and characteristics these people reveal which are similar to your own - human life unfolds as an ever-developing archetype.

So, by way of explanation let us repeat ourselves - our collective conscious has been created from the experience of everyone who has lived - the whole of humanity's history is contained and encapsulated within the atmosphere of our existence - we are the summation of human happening.

There is a gap between your reality and these stories - and if you listen carefully for the silence lying in between, there may be a truth waiting to be heard within the chiming of a bell.

Can you hear it?

Chapter 1 - The Chairman

'The truth of how you live is very rarely the truth of your life.'

It may seem rather peculiar to recommence our narratives with a description of a property - yet within the space where an individual lives and works much may be perceived about them from the quality of their surrounding environment. And so it is with the Chairman - whose primary workspace is an office situated on the top floor of a city centre building situated up a small side street close to the Cathedral in an area recently designated as the 'City Heritage Centre'.

Naturally one would assume being in possession of an address in such an appointed area would bring with it a certain degree of prestige, it does not. Whilst in previous ages the Centre was certainly acknowledged as the place to be seen and do business, this was prior to the great financial crash which brought substantial economic hardship to the type of businesses who had historically gravitated together within the Cathedral quarter.

As a direct result of this economic decline the last two decades have taken their toll on the ageing fabric of the district, and it is the hope of the local unitary authority that by marketing the centre as 'Heritage' more tourists will be attracted to stay in the increasingly rundown, impoverished and overpriced inner city hotels without the need to incur any further 'unnecessary' expenditure to restore the local infrastructure to its previous glory.

Nevertheless, the building in which the Chairman's office resides can hardly be described as neglected. The fabric of the building is Georgian in appearance and, on the face of it, appears to fit comfortably within its dilapidated surrounding neighbourhood. It does not stand out or draw attention to itself in any particular way, yet, in reality, it is home to the most technological, ecologically friendly and self-sustainable working environment coexisting within the somewhat over-populated city in which it resides.

Prior to its current stewardship the property had fallen into rack and ruin under the ownership of an ageing firm of solicitors who could see no point in updating its antediluvian interior - they felt it projected the appropriate image of who and what they were - and indeed it did. The firm collapsed following a grubby little scandal concerning the fraudulent diversion of funds from estates they were managing as executors.

The building was purchased as a personal investment opportunity by the late, much lauded philanthropist, entrepreneur, business angel and Knight of the realm, a person who just also happened to be the Guardian of the teenage boy who would grow up to become the Chairman of a large international corporation and the current occupant of the office on the top floor.

If you have only recently come to our tales then a little reminiscence will not go amiss.

Back at the time of the original acquisition the Guardian was the Acting Chief Executive of RLE Incorporated Limited, a leading international professional services organisation specialising in health, wellbeing, and wellness in the workplace. This was a business he had resurrected on behalf of his ward out of the dying embers of 'The Religion of Least Effort (RLE™)', a quasi-esoteric psychotherapeutic enterprise founded by his ward's parents. The boy's father had been a close school friend of his and shortly prior to his and his wife's untimely and unfortunate demise in an aviation accident whilst travelling in a small charter plane over the rain forest of Borneo, he had agreed, during an alcohol fuelled evening of bonhomie, to be Guardian to their only teenage son in the unlikely event anything should happen to them. The boy, at that time, happened to be a pupil of their old alma mater, The Boarding School.

Whilst, as has been mentioned previously in our tales, the Guardian may have initially regretted the decision made over several vintage bottles of white Burgundy wine, he decided to take his role seriously. As an extremely successful businessman and entrepreneur he had the vision to create something of value out of the rather peculiar legacy bequeathed to his ward. He came out of semi-retirement and developed what essentially evolved into a new, highly reputable and profitable business - RLE Incorporated Limited. He decided to remain as the custodian of this successful enterprise until it could be transferred to his ward following the completion of an appropriate education in business administration.

As the new venture took off and he started to engage more employees than his own existing office space could cater for, the Guardian recognised the potential for acquiring what would become a prestigious office in the city in order to accommodate them. He purchased the run-down city centre building, and financed its first initial renovation, completely gutting the interior and reconfiguring it in a way which would increase its longevity into the future. This also included the construction of a spacious underground car park beneath its curtilage, an essential commodity for attracting potential employees owing to the very limited amount of parking available within the City Heritage Centre. Once the renovations were completed he let out the property to RLE Incorporated Limited on a commercial rent payable to his newly established personal property management company.

As directed the ward dutifully completed the appropriate education, finally achieving a master's degree in business administration from a prestigious North American business school to add to his honours degree in business strategy and economics. He returned from North America to take up his position as chief executive of RLE Incorporated Limited. Under his leadership the company became increasingly successful resulting in a highly profitable merger with ROC Services PLC, a major outsourcing company working primarily within the public sector.

The building remained the headquarters of RLE Incorporated Limited until, a couple of years prior to the merger with ROC Services PLC, the building was no longer capable of accommodating the increasing number of staff being employed. The decision was made to move the head office and the majority of the company's personnel to a trendier location in the new up and coming commercial office park development situated just outside the heart of the city on the bank of the central river.

Following the merger with ROC Services PLC the Chief Executive was persuaded to take on the role of Executive Chairman for the newly created corporation – now known as RLE Services PLC. He accepted the appointment and decided to move from the new headquarters to the office he had previously occupied in the old Georgian building. The building was still home to the company secretary, the legal division, and the corporate accountancy team - all the departments responsible for maintaining shareholder value and stakeholder expectations and who would, from now on, be reporting primarily to the Chairman.

So it made sense for him to return to the old building to be closer to those departments directly under his control. And it is during these last few years he has overseen and supervised the final renovations required to elevate the building toward its current ecologically friendly and energetically efficient state.

He is now both owner and landlord having inherited the property management company following the death of the Guardian. At some point in the future, when he finally retires, he plans to convert the building into an art studio and public gallery and these final renovations will realise its inspiration. He himself is an exceptionally fine draughtsman and has always dreamt that one day he would be involved within the arts in some capacity or other.

He had originally intended to study art curation and administration at university, however, his Guardian advised against it and propelled him towards the qualifications which would enable him to make the most from his parent's legacy and conduct a successful career in business - as the Guardian repeatedly advised him - 'you can make a foray into the world of art later in life when you have made enough money to do whatever you want'.

Whilst the Chairman has indeed become exceedingly wealthy over the years, he has yet to turn his dream into reality. The problem is he can never quite find the right time to step away from the business which has preoccupied his life for so many years, and, of course, there is always tomorrow.

It is 6.21am when he arrives at the door of his office. He pauses for a moment, places his hand over the biometric palm reader and registers the click as the door lock opens. He presses the handle downwards with his right hand as he pushes the door forward gently. As he passes under the door frame, he stops, looks across the light oak wood panelled room and registers the pile of daily newspapers awaiting his perusal placed tidily in a fan shape on top of his pale ash work desk by the early duty concierge before his arrival.

The office he has returned to is smaller than the one he had formerly occupied as Chief Executive in the new headquarters - the dimensions are 26 foot 1 inch by 16 foot 4 inches. The wall opposite the door has three large Georgian windows facing out over the narrow street. The desk is set at an angle in the left-hand corner, away from the wall giving the occupant a view of the whole office. On the right-hand side of the office there is a small meeting table with the capacity to seat six. This table is very similar to the one he had previously commissioned for his headquarter office, though less than half the size - it is constructed in the same pale ash wood as his desk - plain and simple in design but with intricate inlays of vines flowing through the legs and around the edge of the table. It is possible you would not notice them at first as they seem barely visible to the eye, but the more you look at them, the more they appear to come alive as if blowing in a morning breeze. Around this table are placed six chairs.

Against the wall opposite to the desk and adjacent to the door there is a small refreshment unit - constructed in the same pale ash wood. On top of this unit there is a metal bowl containing one apple, pear, peach and plum, next to a bronze combination thermal kettle, positioned close to a wooden tray on which there are placed four artisanal handmade craft mugs and an ash wood open top box containing a selection of his favourite herbal teas.

He sighs, walks across to the refreshment unit, checks there is water in the kettle and sets it to boil. He then moves over to his Burgundy red antique

Gainsborough office chair positioned carefully behind his desk, sits down, moves the papers to one side, and retrieves a very old and battered looking soft brown leather A2 size portfolio case from the cabinet filing drawer built into the left-hand side of the desk. He opens the case, pulls out a sheet of top quality 200-gram acid free A3 sized paper, a box containing a selection of artist pencils and charcoals and places them in front of him. He takes a moment to become aware of his breathing, finds sensation within his body and begins to sketch.

He first started sketching as a pastime when he was six years old. It was the Aunt (a retired primary school headteacher) who encouraged him. She had been employed to care for him during the school holidays as his parents were far too preoccupied with developing their own career as as psycho-spiritual gurus to look after him outside term time away from his boarding school. Consequently, he lived with her in her little two-bedroom housing association bungalow within the leafy suburbs of the somewhat overpopulated city.

The Aunt was quite particular about how children should engage with the world around them, and this was certainly not through the screen of a television or any other such media - drawing, along with educational games, creative writing and storytelling were the only ways in which, in her mind, children should be enlivened in preparation for a useful human existence.

He continued to live with the Aunt after his parents died - it was an arrangement made between her and the Guardian who, with two young daughters of a similar age to the ward, had some concern over pubescent hormones running riot within his own household. She was more than happy to continue the arrangement - the boy had become for her the child she had never had.

He finally left what had become his home when he started university. It wasn't a formal decision made by either of them - it just happened. The university was in another city, and it was more convenient for him to take lodgings there. After graduating from university he moved to North America to study at the internationally renowned business school. Although the aunt kept his room as it had always been he never returned to live with her.

Nevertheless, he maintained contact visiting her regularly - he regarded her as a beloved relative, a valued friend and wise mentor. It was he who provided her with the financial support she needed during her final years and it was he who arranged the private care package to ensure she could live out her days in her own home - the bungalow in which she had resided for nigh on seventy years and which he had purchased on her behalf from the housing association many years previously. It was his way of saying thank you for the beneficial influence and significant role she had played in his development as a human being.

In some ways he always thought the Aunt would live forever – she had been an ever present feature in his life. So he was quite shocked when she finally died just less than a month ago. He had not been informed of the death until after her cremation – her legal representative told him she had wanted a simple, no fuss cremation. The solicitor then went on to inform him he had been appointed as her sole executor - she had also left him a letter containing some very detailed instructions as to the disposal of her ashes – he would find it on the dining table in the living room of her bungalow. The solicitor has arranged to meet him later today.

In many respects it was the Aunt who had nurtured his creativity and intellectual stability, whilst it was the Guardian had cultivated the business and financial acumen for which he is more generally known.

Nevertheless, regardless of his undoubtable success in the world of commerce, anyone who has contemplated upon his primary works of art (for there are a few on public display) will advise you that his attention to detail is exquisite and he exhibits a refined skill in their execution.

The early morning sketches, such as the one he is undertaking at the moment, are much simpler in execution – it is a ritual meditation he has undertaken every single morning since first attending university. These drawings which appear to evolve from the inner recesses of his subconscious are purely personal, more akin to a doodle; yet within these lines there is a message to be perceived. Whatever picture emanates from this vigil will set the theme for the day together with a question to be considered.

At 6.53 am he moves his eyes away from the sheet of paper he has been drawing on and places the piece of charcoal he has just been using back onto the desk beside the other pencils and charcoals. He sits upright in the chair, placing his hands palm upwards on his thighs, closes his eyes and undertakes a journey around his body. He then remains listening to his silence for a several plus one excursions of his heart. It is then he chooses to scrutinise the picture he has drawn. He sighs for a second time.

He has created a caricature of a man probably in his early to mid-fifties with a full head of light grey hair parted to the right and trimmed just above the ear. The man is relatively handsome - however, his face is racked with pain. Sticking into his neck, as if forcibly placed there by another person, is an object - it is this image which has generated the deep exhalation of air from his lungs. The object is none other than his company's logo - a black cross, bearing an intricate vine traced within it, resting on a six-pointed star, partially enclosed within a circle.

The company logo is also the map on which the 'Symbolic Psychometric Personality Assessment™' is formulated. This unique assessment tool enables the identification of an individual's personality type together with an indication of the type of activity they are most suited to and which would give them the greatest satisfaction in their life. He personally oversaw the development of this product and he considers it to be his lasting legacy. He has always felt the 'Symbolic Psychometric Personality Assessment™' has the potential to ease many of the world's humanitarian concerns regarding the full and satisfactory employment of its citizens. As the well-worn and highly successful PR mantra concludes -

'Using the timeless wisdom of the ancient philosophers, refined by the leading psychologists of the day, The 'Symbolic Psychometric Personality Assessment™' *enables everyone to easily understand their preferences for*

life and work and determine the necessary actions to achieve inner self-contentment in all they do.'

Following the merger with ROC Services PLC the new company RLE Services PLC has continued to successfully promote this product on a worldwide basis. In the UK, partly because of the large number of outsourced public sector services managed previously by ROC Services PLC, it has become the central government's psychometric assessment tool of choice and is currently employed by the company on the government's behalf to assist in the restructuring of the public sector, using it to fit the right people into the right job and identify those who would be more suitably employed elsewhere.

Personally, he considers the adoption of 'his' tool by government to be a double edged sword - whilst it is now widely recognised and universally adopted by the human resources community at large, he is not convinced it is being executed or utilised in a way conducive to his unique utopian vision. However, since his appointment as Executive Chairman he no longer has much influence over the practical day-to-day operations of the business. This responsibility lies with the current Chief Executive - his previous Company Secretary and head of Legal Services at RLE Incorporated Ltd. He has been promoted to the role following the untimely death brought on by a myocardial infarction of the previous Chief Executive (who had held the same role with ROC Services PLC) less than seven months following the merger.

He leans forward, picks up his drawing and places it to the left-hand side of his desk, he takes up the charcoals and pencils and places them back in the box, he then moves the daily newspapers towards him. He pauses as if he is about to look at them but then decides not to do so for the moment and instead stands up and walks towards the small refreshment storage unit

He checks the heat of the water in the kettle, places a mint tea tisane into a mug, and pours the water from the kettle onto it. He watches the sachet start to absorb the liquid and the water gently take on the light green sheen indicating the readiness of flavour he particularly prefers.

He returns to his desk, sits down and places the beverage on top of a RLE Services PLC coaster bearing the company insignia. It is then he notices the front page of the local city gazette. On the front cover there is a photograph of the man he has just drawn smiling out at him underneath the caption - 'Unemployed actor murdered by his ex job coach'.

He reads the leading paragraph and then turns to page five where the story is recounted in detail. Murders are a rare event in the city and the gazette rarely has something so 'exciting' to report to its readership.

According to the paper the 'actor' had been working for the local unitary authority customer services unit where following an organisational review undertaken by RLE Services PLC he was made redundant. He had met the 'job coach' at his back to work interview at the city unemployment claimants office - evidently he had been upset about the way in which the interview was conducted. By coincidence and shortly there-afterwards, she became unemployed from her frontline facing role following an organisational review of her office undertaken by RLE Services PLC - she had disliked the job she was transferred to and resigned her post. Since then she had been unable to find an employer who would take her on. The two antagonists accidentally came across each other in the Four Feathers, a rundown public house situated in the suburbs of the city. Following an argument she had thrust a broken pint glass into his throat. Whilst she had claimed it was an accident, she has been found guilty and sentenced to a life term in prison.

There then followed an interview with a local area union representative - both the 'actor' and the 'job coach' had belonged to the same public sector union. The union representative questioned the integrity of the reviews undertaken by RLE Services PLC and the validity of utilising the 'Symbolic Psychometric Personality Assessment™' (SPPA) as a tool for determining redundancies. The union representative is quoted as saying -

'I find it surprising that a psychometric assessment tool purporting to help people achieve inner self-contentment in the work they do is used by the

public sector in a way that has resulted in the death of one person and ruined the life of another.'

Evidently RLE Services PLC has released a statement -

'The company offers its condolences to all those affected by this tragedy. Nevertheless, we cannot make any detailed or personal comment on individual contracts undertaken on behalf of the public sector - they are confidential. However, we would point out that the 'Symbolic Psychometric Personality Assessment™' has been subjected to highest level of academic research by leading psychologists. This research has been published internationally and subjected to rigorous peer review. As a result the 'Symbolic Psychometric Personality Assessment™' is considered the 'platinum standard' in psychometric assessment for both personal and organisational use.'

He reads the statement a second time and then a third time. He is not sure he can believe what he is reading. Certainly no-one had made him aware of this incident. He should have been informed - he was the Chairman after all and an affair such as this, which could well impact on the share value of the business, should have been brought to his attention.

He looks at the sketch he has just drawn and sighs for a third time.

That the Chairman displays a prophetic gift which is revealed within his artistic works of imagination is widely acknowledged amongst the very few people who have any knowledge of his character and history. Indeed most of those who consider him of close familiarity find his creative meanderings quite disturbing in their markedly unsettling accuracy in revealing an unsuspected happening.

Nevertheless, he is more than aware his visionary gift has never been fully consummated for he has not once been able to divine the actual future from any of the pictures he has drawn, they simply come into existence and the veracity revealed within many of them only manifests its being after the event. For example, this morning's sketch relates to a past occurrence he was simply unaware of and for the moment he has no cognisance with regard to the ongoing reality of its meaning.

Everyone on this little planet of yours experiences, from one time or another, an emotional shock of some sort - we observe them frequently. How you react to even the smallest of these psychological crises depends on the life you have lived. It may shift slightly the range of your habitual perceptions - though possibly only for a short term. For example, a friend or close acquaintance unexpectedly draws upon their last breath and the bell ceases to chime for them - and for a few days, conscious of the fragility of your own mortality, you walk just a little more carefully and ponderously as you go about your daily business.

Occasionally an emotional shock fundamentally changes how you interrelate and cohabitate within your world. In this particular scenario the Chairman suffers accordingly.

He finds himself sitting in his seat a little more firmly than before. He feels a wave of emotion spreading like the incoming tide across the whole of his body moving upwards from his feet and downwards from his head. When the various waves of emotion finally catch up with each other and crossover within his solar plexus he feels a new sensation - the sensation of a lie. It moves upwards through his body. He can taste its bitterness as it passes up through his chest and into his mouth. He can smell it in his nostrils. He can feel the prickle in the roots of his hair. Suddenly he feels alive and alert, as if he has just received a high energy electrical shock to his nervous system.

Then there is a sensation of nausea and loss as he suddenly recognises he is not who he thought he was - he has been inhabiting a dream world of his own creation. He had always prided himself as someone who operated with the highest levels of self-awareness, now he realises he has been asleep to the reality of what he has become.

The realisation floods within his being as he begins to rapidly make sense of what has been going on around him.

He has been blinded by his own arrogance and the sentiments of self-importance accumulated over the years as the head of a company he is no longer in control of. He has allowed himself to be kept outside of the day-to-day operations of a business he and his Guardian had built over many years. He has become a powerless figurehead indulgently permitted to come into his office and pretend to be a something he is not. Yes, he had fallen into a habitual way of existence and the life in which he conceives himself to be living with a degree of awareness is merely an illusion. He has been a lie unto himself and has not recognised the truth of his own existence. And, as he breathes deeply into his diaphragm he acknowledges a simple fact - he does not actually know what that particular truth is - he no longer knows who or what he is. He sighs again for the fourth time and falls into a numbed daze of melancholic inertia.

He cannot believe what has happened but the only conclusion he can come to is that the whole of the senior management team and the board have lied to him through omission. He has not been informed of this story or the company's response. He has been kept out of the loop regarding this incident. Yes – although he is a major shareholder in the business he has lost any influence he ever had over the company's day to day business operations.

There is a knock on the door.

The Chairman is immediately drawn out of his stupor - he is not expecting a visitor. He automatically moves his right arm towards his face, turns his wrist and looks at his watch - it is 7.03 am and far too early in the day for his personal assistant to arrive.

He pauses in thought for a moment and before he has a chance to ask 'who is it?', the door opens and a middle aged man, lean with dark slick backed hair, neatly groomed beard, and wearing a dark suit over an expensive looking open necked white linen shirt, enters.

Immediately forgetting all he has just experienced the Chairman instinctively smiles at the entree with a degree of pleasure and surprise - the other duly smiles back.

His visitor is none other than the Chief Executive, a man he has known since recruiting him from university after he had successfully completed his LLB (Hons). It was the Chairman who encouraged him to specialise in business law and mentored him into his previous role as Company Secretary and Head of Legal Services. Over the years he has grown particularly fond of him recognising him as a highly competent operator and advisor - in fact his natural successor.

"Good morning, I was just passing by and thought I would pop in and see how you are doing. May I sit down for a moment?"

The Chairman registers a similar sensation of emotion flowing through his body as he had just experienced after reading the article. He instinctively knows the man in front of him is lying. He was not 'just passing', there was an ulterior purpose behind this visit. He could taste something behind the spoken words and there was a grey cloud swirling around the sound of his speech like the myst of a damp dull and somewhat heavy morning.

Obviously, the 'just passing', on the face of it would not normally be considered a 'big' or 'evil' lie in anyway - however, the feeling engendered in the Chairman indicated something unpropitious lay behind this visit - something infelicitous.

He looks at the Chief Executive and acquiesces.

The Chief Executive smiles and walks across the room towards the meeting table room and removes one seat, walks back across the room and places it at the opposite side of the desk in front of the Chairman.

"Would you like a drink?" The Chairman asks politely. "The kettle has just boiled." He points towards the refreshment unit.

"Thank you and no thank you - as I said I am only passing."

Again, the spoken words engender the same unpleasant feeling within the Chairman's body. Nevertheless, he smiles at the Chief Executive.

"I have known you long enough to be more than aware you never pass any location by accident. Why are you here? Anything to do with this perhaps?" The Chairman points to the front headline of the local city gazette.

"Partly - I guessed you would see the story in our local rag this morning and I just wanted to assure you everything is in hand."

The Chairman looks toward the Chief Executive. "I have to admit to being somewhat surprised I was not informed about this. I appreciate I am no longer engaged or responsible for the daily operational activities of the business, however, it is I who am answerable to the shareholders, and represent their interests, especially if anything happens - for example a story such of this relating to one of our most profitable products - one which could potentially reduce the value of our stock."

The Chief Executive does not reply but looks across the desk at the Chairman. The Chairman can see by the look on the Chief Executive's face he is struggling to find a suitable reply - one which would pacify him.

All of a sudden the Chief Executive notices the sketch on the desk and immediately draws backwards into his chair. Instinctively he moves his left hand over his mouth. After a moment he moves forwards from his seat to consider the sketch more closely. As he does so he becomes increasingly self-conscious and slowly moves his hand away from his mouth, down over his chin, returning it to its habitual resting place, palm downwards on the upper part of his left thigh. He lifts his right hand and points casually toward the picture.

"May I assume you drew this before you read the story in the paper?" He asks cautiously, being more than aware of the Chairman's artistic proclivity.

"You may," replies the Chairman.

The Chief Executives smiles - somewhat ruefully. "May I also assume your interest has been somewhat piqued?"

The Chairman smiles back. "Well, if it wasn't it certainly has been now, especially as you are in my office having just 'passed by' my door at a time especially early, even for you, to visit anyone…

"We have worked closely together ever since I recruited you to our fast-track graduate programme from university. I saw your potential and I have nurtured your career. You are bothered about something and you are not being honest with me. I can smell it in the air and I can certainly feel it in my bones. You do not want me involved with this in anyway."

He pauses for a moment and scrutinises the Chief Executive's face searching for some sort of validation to the proposed thesis he has just proffered. Not finding the answer he was looking for, he continues.

"As you are more than aware the SPPA was my project, I initiated it and as far as I am concerned it is my personal responsibility - it is one of the most important and practical contributions I have made to this business. Its creation led to our merger with ROC Services PLC, albeit indirectly. Not only has it provided a living for ourselves and our employees, within it lies the potential to make world a better place in which to live…"

He pauses, feeling a sensation of nausea pulsate within his solar plexus and chest - it rises up and down his body. For a moment he perceives lines of dark stars flashing dully in front of his eye. He becomes aware he has just spoken a lie and deep down in his solar plexus and has an overwhelming realisation he can no longer continue live the life he has allowed to manifest within his own peculiar dream of a utopian world.

He feels the weight of his words hanging listlessly in the air - he can see they have no life - no movement - no authenticity. His treasured legacy has possibly led to the death of one person and destroyed the life of another. He needs to discover the actual reality hiding behind the psychometric tool he has been responsible for building.

"Are you ok?" The Chief Executive notices the momentary expression of anguish on the Chairman's face.

"No - something is very clearly wrong when an idea promoting wellness in the workplace and the overall betterment of society results in the death of one person and the imprisonment of another. It was never my intention for the SPPA to be used in a way which would result in harming the people undertaking it."

The Chief Executive sighs almost imperceptibly and smiles benevolently toward the Chairman - it is an unintentional gesture on the part of the Chief Executive.

The Chairman notices the movement and immediately identifies with it - it is the indulgent smile of an adult believing themselves to be communicating with a child.

It suddenly becomes apparent to him the man opposite no longer respects him as a business equal - something in their relationship has changed - a connection which used to exist between them has been broken. The balance of power between them has shifted.

He ponders the situation for a moment and tries to discern when the change in their relationship had occurred. Was it following the Chief Executive's recent divorce? Certainly, ever since then the man had become increasingly distant – he no longer confided with him as he had in the past.

The Chairman had chosen not to discuss the matter at the time – as far as he was concerned the marital difficulties of his prodigy was none of his business – if the man wished to discuss it he would surely raise it and then he would have happily talked through any personal issues he was experiencing with him

Nevertheless, he had observed the Chief Executive become increasingly obsessed with maintaining the ongoing profitability and successful management of the business. He had assumed at the time the Chief Executive's fixation was merely a temporary displacement activity to divert his attention away from what was progressively becoming a bitter and acrimonious estrangement from his wife. Now he is no longer sure – something else has been going on behind his back.

24

He looks at the Chief Executive waiting for him to respond.

The Chief Executive continues to smile until realising the Chairman is looking at him in a quizzical manner. He consciously changes his facial expression to one he calculates will convey affable concern.

"Don't you think you may be overreacting just a little?" The smile returns. "To be honest this is why I 'passed by' - I knew you would feel this way and I need to reassure you there is no conceivable connection between the SPPA and the deaths."

He pauses for a moment and intentionally makes direct eye contact with the Chairman.

"Clearly whatever happened was the result of a pitiful squabble between two poor inebriated souls in a squalid public house which tragically got out of hand. We can hardly blame the SPPA or the excellent work of our consultants for something as unforeseeable as this? My team have got the situation in hand, it is an operational matter and is unlikely to have any impact on our shareholders. It's not an issue for you to be involved with in any way. It will all be forgotten about within a day or two." He pauses again as he notices the Chairman wince.

"What's wrong?" He asks.

"I am sorry but I am not prepared to forget about it." The Chairman replies. "To do so would go against my principles and all I have worked to achieve for this business. The SPPA was my legacy and, as I just said, I feel accountable for how it is being used and perceived by the people using it.

"As you well know my Guardian, the man who essentially set up RLE from the residual legacy left by my parents, was a great philanthropist. He tried to instil in me the same values that his father had instilled in him - primarily to never forget where you came from and treat everyone and everything with the deepest respect, especially in business.

"He specifically wanted something of benefit to come out of my parents' untimely death. We are the heirs to his work and we are responsible for the integrity of his business. I chose to explore the meaning behind the logo my parents had chosen as their marketing brand - the one we still use to this day. When we ascertained the symbolism it contained within its design I was able to evolve the meaning into something which would be advantageous to the world - something else of benefit to come out of my parents' death."

He looks across at the Chief Executive to ensure he has his full and undivided attention.

"There is a fatal flaw within my legacy - an error in its application and I intend to find out the truth of the error and rectify it. Do you know the development of SPPA was the only matter my Aunt and I ever disagreed over. She was never happy about our use of the symbol for business purposes and she was adamant our interpretation of the symbol was fundamentally flawed. She was never prepared to discuss it other than say matters of the spiritual realm should stay within that realm and certainly had no place within a commercial setting. I argued the spiritual dimension was equally important in business and it was the only way in which the world would become a better place. She considered my response naive and I chose to ignore her concerns. Whilst she expressed her disappointment we let the matter lie. Maybe she did know something we didn't. Anyway I need to find out."

The Chief Executive pauses before responding.

"I only met her the once. She was an amiable old soul and I was sorry to hear of your recent loss, but I doubt she could have known very much about our research. The studies into the origins of the Symbol were professionally undertaken - you insisted on that and I ensured it happened. The psychological methodology underpinning the development of SPPA has been fully peer reviewed, and time and time again the ongoing research has validated the assessment process. The last thing our business needs right now is a chairman questioning the veracity of one of his company's leading products and income generators."

An uncomfortable silence falls between the Chief Executive and the space separating him from the Chairman. The Chief Executive appears to be weighing carefully how he should proceed with this dialogue. Eventually his mind is made up.

"Whilst you and your guardian's daughters are key shareholders in this business you no longer hold a majority. You are in post at the behest of the shareholders - a figurehead to acknowledge the history of the company. Shareholders can be fickle, especially if they believe the value of the business is being detrimentally impacted by the behaviour of their chairman. The share value of the business has very little to do with philanthropy. For your own sake please trust me to deal with this."

The Chairman looks at the younger man. He begins to recognise the gulf between them has grown much larger than he would ever have anticipated. It had been his decision to promote this person as his successor and his recommendation had been accepted by the board and shareholders. He had assumed the Chief Executive would naturally want to follow the line of the path he had set out for the business - it was now obvious he was following his own.

"I have always trusted you, especially with regard to the interests of our company. But I now recognise we are different in temperament. I want to know the truth - I wish to find the truth - I wish people to live in truth. I am not convinced you want what I want in this matter. Maybe the interests of the business no longer reflect mine. Don't you want to know the truth?" The Chairman looks toward the Chief Executive in askance.

"My dear William," replies the Chief Executive, "therein lies the arrogance - it sits within your wish. Most people do not understand the concept of truth let alone seek to find it. I am not sure I even know what the truth is. The world, and certainly our world in business, relies on a degree of misperception and misconception in order to survive. Is that a truth? Could our business survive in a world of truth?

"I am more than aware I will not be able to dissuade you from following whatever path you determine to take. However, if you wish to pursue this matter please don't claim to be doing it on behalf of the company - take a sabbatical - you deserve one. You need a break. I can inform the board you are taking a six-month sabbatical with immediate effect. For the short term I will act as Chair in your absence. However, for my sake, please don't rock the boat and keep me informed of anything you discover which may impact on the business. I seriously doubt you will find anything of import."

For a moment the Chairman is stunned by what he has just heard. He feels an unanticipated sense of isolation and abandonment. Has he just been fired from his own company?

"Maybe you should clarify your last comment. It does not sound like a request but a foregone conclusion I am to take a sabbatical."

The Chief Executive frowns.

"You need to remember this is no longer the business you and your guardian created - of course what you built is still a part of what exists today, but RLE Services PLC has grown way beyond what your old business could ever have achieved. It requires a different style of management and we have to move with the times.

"To be honest some of our key stakeholders have begun to question privately whether or not you have been at the helm of our ship for too long. They wonder if the company has grown too large for you. The business is so much more than the SPPA - there is all the outsourcing work we are doing for the government in the prisons and health service. There is our international reputation.

"I truly believe in your abilities and after a short respite from the daily strictures of office life I am sure you will return refreshed. However, if you don't take some time off I cannot guarantee there will not be a move to replace you. Do this for yourself and for the business. I appreciate this may have come as a shock so I will leave you now. But please will you contact me with a decision before the end of a day."

The Chief Executive gets up from the chair, smiles, and walks to the door. As he opens it he turns around.

"I am only doing what any friend would do in this situation."

As the Chief Executive leaves the room the Chairman feels yet another pulsating sense of shock. There is no floor beneath his feet. He is floating through space in a whirl of distortion. He needs to ground himself and return to some sort of reality. He consciously makes the effort to find sensation in his feet.

When he manages to do so he acknowledges to himself that the only way to truly calm himself down is to undertake another meditation. He breathes deeply and retrieves his old and battered soft brown leather A2 size portfolio case. He opens the bag and pulls out a sheet of top quality 200 gram acid free A3 sized paper, the box containing the selection of artist pencils and charcoals, and places them in front of him. He takes a moment to become aware of his breathing and starts to draw.

At 8.03 am he moves his eyes away from the piece of paper he has been drawing on and places the piece of charcoal he has just been using back onto the desk beside the other pencils and charcoals. He again sits upright in the chair, placing his hands palm upwards on his thighs, closes his eyes and undertakes a journey around his body. He then remains listening to his silence for a several plus one excursions of his heart. It is then he chooses to scrutinise the second picture of the day.

He has sketched a portrait of himself as a teenage boy. The boy is standing poised in front of two large pillars looking down a straight path protected on each side by two large brick walls covered with a large vine stretching down along them. It is overcast, shadowy and uninviting. The line of the path and the walls seem to extend into eternity. It appears he is about to place one foot forward and enter through the pillars and onto the path - yet doubts whether he should move forward or not.

He continues to contemplate his drawing allowing an understanding of its meaning to seep gently into his awareness. Slowly but surely it dawns upon him he has been blindly following the line of a path created for him by his guardian - it was not his own path, his path was the one he has just drawn and he is yet to journey consciously along its way.

He meditates on his sketch for a few more minutes, clarifying in his mind the decision he feels in his heart. He picks up the phone and dials a call through to the Chief Executive. He observes himself feeling surprisingly relieved when it immediately transfers to the Chief Executive's voice mail. He speaks slowly and carefully.

"Thank you for coming to see me this morning. It was an interesting conversation and I have thought through what you have said. I will take a sabbatical with immediate effect. I have some duties relating to the death of the Aunt which I need to undertake and so I was planning to take a leave of absence anyway. Please can you make the appropriate arrangements and inform the board and shareholders of my decision in a way which will not provoke any undue concern. We will speak later."

He places the phone back down on the receiver and positions the newspapers in a neat pile on his clean pale ash wood desk, gets up from his Burgundy red antique Gainsborough office chair, picks up his old and battered looking soft brown leather A2 size portfolio case together with the box of artist pencils and charcoals, looks across the light wood panelled room, walks across the office floor and leaves through the door.

Chapter 2 - The Aunt

'It is only in the silence where Truth may be found
hidden away from the noise of your life.'

The Aunt sits quietly beside her dining table in the living room of the small two-bedroom bungalow situated within the leafy suburbs of the somewhat overpopulated city. She is meditating upon a blank sheet of paper. It is finally the time to write the letter she has been composing in her mind during the sleepless nights brought on from what she knows will be her final illness.

She is feeling very old - but then again she is very old. In many respects she has always felt old - ever since she returned from the Ashram in India although she had only been in her late twenties. She smiles to herself as she considers her decrepitude now in comparison to the person she was then. She has achieved much in her long life and, as she approaches her certain death, has the satisfaction of knowing she lived a good life.

She is about to pick up her ink pen when she pauses for a moment. Yes, she decides - I will allow myself the luxury of a little reminiscence.

She has lived in this old bungalow ever since she returned from her travels and took up her post as a teacher for 'year 6' children at the local and somewhat antiquated Victorian primary school - the one where she would became the venerable and highly respected headmistress at the age of forty-five.

Fifteen years later, she was 'encouraged' to take early retirement by the newly formed unitary authority. The education and social services committee concluded her small successful school provided far too many advantages for its pupils in comparison to those provided within the larger modern purpose built neighbourhood schools, and should therefore be closed with the children transferred to a more egalitarian setting - every child, it was considered, regardless of where they lived, should be given an equal chance to determine their futures, and being educated within a larger educational establishment with a more diverse population and a higher student to teacher ratio would achieve this aim at reduced costs.

It was shortly after her 'retirement' when she developed a reputation as an outstanding minder and private educator to the children of the professionally minded, especially those whose preference was to continue successfully with their own careers unabated by the inconvenience of having to look after their own children.

She enjoyed her part time work immensely as it allowed her more flexibility to teach her charges in a way she considered to be appropriate to life. She gave each child her full attention and ensured they would leave her with the skills, and the knowledge, to be of service in society. Virtually all of the children who were placed in her care (of course there are a few exceptions) remember her fondly and appreciate the deep impression she has made on their life. Over the years she became affectionately known as the Aunt.

She finally gave up her 'part time' occupation some ten years ago when it became apparent to her prospective non-parentally inclined clientele that a woman in her nineties, and older than their own children's great grandparents, was probably too elderly to care for their offspring. In reality she had become ageless - her appearance today is much as it was when she was sixty, albeit somewhat shorter in stature as is only natural within the passage of time.

She is now a centenarian, and whilst not as lithe as in previous years, she is still more than capable of maintaining herself, the bungalow and garden with a little support from a carer who comes in every morning and evening to check in on her. She is one of the world's more fortunates who are blessed with both a healthy mind and attitude towards her toilette and diet. Food should be wholesome and pure - preferably home grown and most certainly prepared by herself freshly every day. This lifelong discipline, along with many others, evolved in her twenties whilst residing as a visitor for several months in a beautiful Ashram by the side of the River Ganges.

It was there she developed an intuitive appreciation for the principles behind Ayurveda which she applied ever afterwards in her daily living. All the food needed to nourish the residents was grown in the gardens around the Ashram and she learnt much about their cultivation by assisting the long-term residents who worked the land on a daily basis.

Likewise, she acquired great deal of knowledge from helping the cooks in the kitchen concerning the proper preparation of food together with the appropriate use of herbs and spices to balance the doshas. It was also at the Ashram where she developed her enduring respect for eastern philosophy, esoteric practices, meditation and yoga. Everything she learnt was integrated, through attention and intention, into the very fabric of her being, and freely passed on through osmosis to all those she cared for.

Although by nature a humble person, she is proud of the fact that at the age of 103 years she can look after herself with a minimal amount of support from anyone else. She is not extravagant although the few garments she possesses are of an existential quality - couture tailored to last and were purchased whilst she was still employed as a head teacher. She does allow herself what she considers to be her one and only luxury - a home visit from a young hairdresser (a person she had once minded) every four weeks to 'tidy up' her exuberant crop of silver white hair. Her hair turned white very unexpectedly following her return from India. She did not suffer the vanity of needing to dye it back to the original dark chestnut and the hair has blessed her in return by remaining in the pleasure of her company.

Equally she has never really cared about her looks - she never condescended to the use of any cosmetics or perfumes. Nevertheless, she portrays a Pre-Raphaelite fineness in her countenance, consistently exuding a brightness of being which makes her beautiful to behold without her even realising it. Although now somewhat smaller of stature her presence fills any space she enters. Her eyes sparkle, not mischievously or with a sense of fun, but rather with a perception of deep awareness and understanding. Her role in life has been to nourish all who come to her with love and compassion.

Of course not everyone she has been responsible for have wished to receive the sustenance held within the commodious store of her knowledge, or to drink the refreshing waters from the existential well of her understanding. She realised this and it never concerned her vanity - under no circumstance would she force the unsolicited blessings of her life onto another against their will, and yet everyone who met her had the opportunity to receive the gift of her presence even though it might be many years before they realise the gift they had received or opened the package of love she left with them.

She picks up her pen and finding it devoid of ink, gets up from her chair and walks slowly over to the old Victorian mahogany sideboard she had inherited from her long since departed parents. She opens the top left-hand drawer and removes a bottle of lavender coloured ink. Having unscrewed the top of the bottle she carefully refills her fountain pen and replaces the bottle back into the drawer. She pauses for a moment to look up at the picture of the old wizened oak tree standing in a courtyard garden hanging above the sideboard. She returns to the dining table and sits down in front of the blank sheet of paper. Yes - she needs to write this letter to the boy who drew the picture, the person who many years ago she came to regard as 'the child she never had'.

Being an only child herself she has no living relatives. She has never married - though she had 'fallen in love', whatever that meant, whilst she was in India. She smiled at the memory. No, to remain within the love of Kamadeva was not to be her destiny. Instead, she was to be the conduit of a different type of love to the numerous number of children who came within her orbit. Now all the children had left - all except the boy who had grown up to become a successful business entrepreneur.

The boy had spent many hours at this very table drawing. It was a gift she had recognised and encouraged from an early age. He was a skilled draughtsman and still talked of one day following his art. Many of his pictures still adorn the walls of her bungalow - the oak tree hanging above the dresser is one of her favourites - it captures a truth and a depth of feeling so often absent in the art of the day.

She has heard the chiming of the bell within the depths of her being calling the changes in the last circle of her life. It is now incumbent on her to 'set her house in order'. She has completed a last will and testament with her solicitor and it is the boy she has named as her sole executor. She needs explain her wishes in a way in which he will understand precisely what is required of him.

There is to be a simple funeral at the crematorium which she has already paid for and he will be required to collect the ashes for disposal according to the instructions set out within the letter she is about to write - her remains are to be sprinkled on the holy waters of the river Ganges next to the Ashram in which she had stayed as a young woman using the monies she has reserved for this purpose. While he is there, for she intends him to deliver her ashes in person, he is to explore the deeper significance contained within the symbol his company appropriated as their business logo many years ago.

It had been his parents who first adopted it for their pseudo psychological spiritual organisation, The Religion of Least Effort (RLE™). The symbol itself is an artistic representation of a cross hanging above the altar in the Church of Universal Values - an independent church of no official denomination set within the very same overpopulated city in which she lives.

The cross in the church was in fact a copy of another cross which was housed within the temple associated with the Ashram she stayed in all those years ago. It was not actually a Christian symbol at all but one of much older origin and tradition. At the church the cross had been set on a backing of cream Italian marble shaped in the form of a six-pointed star made from six interconnecting lines partially enclosed within a silver circle. The original priest and philosopher who founded the Church of Universal values had studied its provenance under the guidance of the Guru who was the spiritual leader of the very same Ashram at the time she had visited it.

It was no coincidence she returned to the same city in which the church was situated - she was aware of its lineage and wished to continue practising a faith aligned to her own experiences of the Ashram. It was at the church where she first met the boy's maternal grandmother and grandfather and they became very close friends.

They had died very shortly following his birth as indeed had his maternal grandparents. The mother and father had both attended the same church for a little while although she never really got to know them well.

However, because of her friendship with the grandparents, and because of her reputation as a child minder, they asked her to care for their son during the school holidays as they were far too busy caring for their business to be able to care for their son at the same time. It was an arrangement which suited her well as it provided a much needed additional source of income. And so the boy came to live with her during holidays and was boarded at school during term time. This arrangement was continued by the boy's Guardian after the parents died in a plane crash.

It was probably only natural for the Guardian to continue using the logo for the business he was essentially setting up for the boy out of the remains of 'The Religion of Least Effort (RLE™). Nevertheless, when the boy had taken over the business he had attributed a meaning to the symbol which was simply not truthful and was potentially dangerous if used incorrectly. He had allowed this meaning to be adapted into a psychometric assessment tool which was now being marketed successfully on a global basis. The use of the symbol for the pecuniary benefit of his business was the only matter over which they ever had anything remotely that could be construed as a disagreement - it was not an argument, yet she felt the issue had created a rift between them. She needed to set the record straight - it would be for his own good.

She is more than aware the boy reminds her of the 'lover' - though not similar in looks he displays a kindred essence within his energy - he has grown into a gentle man. She does not believe this has impacted in her relationship with him in anyway although she has always felt an affinity toward him which she never felt toward the other children she minded.

Anyway the 'lover' has long entered a distant memory. Ever since she left the Ashram she has had no contact with him other than the very occasional letter. She has not heard from him now for many years, yet she believes he is still alive for she would certainly have felt a loss within her had he died.

She smiles as she remembers the touch of his hands and the gentleness of his lips. Whilst their time together and the relationship they shared was embedded within her in the present she is more than aware that to luxuriate inside the feelings she had experienced in the past was not appropriate to her life now. She had put away her feelings - they were merely the lifeless dreams of long-lost days.

She met the 'lover' at the Ashram. He was six years younger than her and she immediately considered him as a 'child' in relation to her obvious maturity as a young woman.

He had arrived at the Ashram two years previously to her and the ancient self-realised saint and master who was the Guru had acknowledged him as having the potential to be a 'seeker of truth'. The 'child' was appointed to be her guardian for the duration of her visit. She found this highly amusing and was equally amused by the earnest seriousness worn on his face on a daily basis as he undertook his responsibilities towards her.

It transpired his father was the pastor of the Church of Universal Values in the somewhat overpopulated city from whence she had arrived. Evidently his grandfather, the founder of the church, had lived and worked at the Ashram in the far distant past.

At the time she was not particularly interested in these minor details. She was soaking up the living experience of her own personal spiritual development under the guidance of the enlightened self-realised saint - her Guruji. Nevertheless, she could not fail to recognise the simple reality the young man she thought of as a child was becoming increasingly infatuated with her and found her sexually appealing.

To begin with she ignored the situation; then she found it rather humorous; and then, because it appealed to her vanity to be found alluring by a 'young' man, she started to play along with it. Without any comprehension of what was happening within her biologically she discovered herself becoming deeply attracted to him on a physical, intellectual, emotional and spiritual level. Consequently they used each and any excuse to spend time together whether it was working in the garden, in the kitchens, or studying the spiritual texts within the Ashram's library.

Of course the deepening aspects of their relationship was obvious to all around them - it is easier to see from the outside what is truly going on within the inside, and they were deeply on the inside oblivious to the smiles and the knowing looks of their fellow travellers.

Then one day the Guruji asked to see them. It was soon to be the festival of Holi, he explained, and it was the tradition of the Ashram to send any European guests to the city together to both experience the festival and to collect various items required for the ongoing maintenance of the Ashram.

Following the Guruji's instructions they checked into the small but comfortable hostel and immediately set about fulfilling the obligations the Guruji required of them. Afterwards they went through the streets of the city towards the river to experience the festivities. It was on their return to the hostel when the arrow of Kamadeva finally struck faithfully on target and their love was consummated.

They returned to the Ashram feeling abashed, guilty and confused - surely what had transpired between them was spiritually sinful. They decided to atone for their obvious transgression and confess all their deeds to the Guruji. He listened to them silently, then looked toward them benevolently and smiled.

"It was the festival of Holi so one should always expect to find Kamadeva playing with his bow and arrows - he particularly likes targeting my European guests - for this is not the first time and it will probably not be the last." He started giggling for a moment as if recalling some amusing memory from the past.

He returned to his gentle smile and continued. "There is no 'sin' as you would say in your traditions. You have experienced one aspect of humanity, one which all should experience at least once in their life. The communion of pleasure between consenting couples is to be truly treasured and honoured. It only 'misses the mark' so to speak when one or the other becomes identified within their own lust and seeks purely to gratify their own sexual urges without the consideration of the other. Alas in the ordinary world this 'sin' occurs more often than it should, even between those who have undertaken a spiritual ritual symbolising sacred union."

Hearing an implicit approval from the Guruji, over the next three weeks they carefully explored this personal communion of pleasure a further three times. It was a period of closeness and personal discovery - a journey they made together. Then the time finally arrived for her to leave the Ashram and return home.

As is often the case in these matters of intimate destiny, on the day of her departure, they expressed their undying love for each other, promising one day they would meet again and remain forever within each other's company - it was not their fate to do so in the way they originally envisaged.

Over the years she has come to realise her memory of events were probably tarnished with a superior quality than the actuality of what really occurred. Nevertheless, her experiences with the lover satisfied a longing which was never to be rekindled - there was to be no replenishment from the well of sensuality and she happily dedicated herself to Maa Saraswati - The Goddess of learning, knowledge, creativity, and music, who herself renounced worldly desires.

She smiles to herself and looks up at the old Victorian pendulum wall clock placed just above the dining table. It is coming up to four-o-clock - she has time to write this letter before preparing her afternoon tea. She picks up her pen and starts to write:

My Dearest William...

****

He walked up the garden path holding the urn in his left hand and a set of keys in his right. Although the solicitor had given him the Aunt's set of keys, he used his own to open the door to the old two bedroomed bungalow.

These were the keys the Aunt had entrusted to him when he was nine years old. He smiled as he recalled her voice telling him - 'it is time for you to assume some responsibility in our life together, therefore I am entrusting you with the keys to my home. Look after them carefully, you never know when you may need them.'

At the time he had felt honoured she would trust him in this way, and it confirmed the familial relationship he felt they experienced with each other, a connection which he did not have with his own parents who were far too engaged in their own life to pay any attention to him other than to ensure he was fed and watered, preferably by someone other than themselves.

He had read the will and knew what his responsibilities were. There would be a letter left behind for him on the dining table in the living room which would explain everything in more detail. The will stipulated a simple funeral service at the crematorium - he was to collect the ashes and then dispose of them as instructed in the letter left for him. She had reserved funds especially for this purpose.

The rest of the will was relatively straightforward. After all expenses and taxes had been paid everything was left for him to do with as he wished. The solicitor told him what he already knew - the only asset of any value was the bungalow. The furniture although mostly antique was dilapidated and not likely to be worth any significant amount. There were some exceptionally fine pictures hanging in the spare room, and one of particular quality positioned above an old mahogany Victorian sideboard in the living room - it was of an old wizened oak tree set in the middle of a formal courtyard garden with a Russian vine growing up it.

The pictures had no discernible provenance having not been signed by the artist though obviously they were the work of one person. Each picture had been dated and incorporated the same motif rendered at the bottom right-hand corner - a detailed representation of a vine leaf. Anyway, he would probably know more about the pictures than he did as they were obviously purchased at around the same time he was residing with the Aunt.

He had smiled at the solicitor who obviously found something in his manner disconcerting. Indeed the solicitor had considered a whole manner of circumstances relating to this will as being peculiar but was unable to effectively challenge the old woman's wishes - the Aunt had been of sound mind when she had made it and was very particular about each and every detail contained within it.

She had been found by her care assistant in the bedroom at 8am. According to the coroner the Doctor concluded she had died peacefully in her sleep approximately four hours earlier. The letter had evidently been written the night before and was left in an envelope addressed to him in person with a clear instruction it was not to be removed from the table by anyone other than himself.

He opened the door and looked down the hall to the living room. The door was open and he could see the old pendulum clock on the wall. There was a female blackbird resting on it. The clock had stopped - the long hand rested on the twelfth numeral and the little hand on the fourth. The blackbird started to trill loudly at his intrusion and flew off the clock, down the hall towards him, and flitted over his head. 'Typical' he smiled to himself, 'she probably arranged that particular greeting especially for me.'

He shut the front door behind him and walked slowly down the hall and through the door into the living room. He stood just in front of the table and registered the envelope addressed to him resting there. He then noticed the time displayed on the clock. He smiled again, it had probably stopped at the exact moment she had died. Again, he would have expected nothing less.

He placed the urn he had just collected from the crematorium on the table and picked up the envelope. As he started to open the envelope he heard a whirring sound coming from the clock, followed by the unmistakable sound of the escapement gear coming into play - a melodious and resonant tick tock broke the silence of the room. He smiled again - the Aunt had been welcomed home.

He sat down at the table and took the letter out of the envelope. It was written in her distinctive and beautiful script, and attached to it was another piece of paper, stained with age, but containing a drawing which very clearly was his company's logo - there was the black cross, bearing an intricate vine traced within it, resting on a golden six-pointed star, partially enclosed within circle, however, the circle was not silver. The top of the circle was coloured in gold which merged into silver, then into a creamy white, and finally into black. He studied it for a short while wondering why the Aunt would have attached the picture to the letter. He looked down at the letter and started to read.

My Dearest William

I can see you now, as I have so often before, sitting at the dining room table, and this time you are holding my letter in your hand. I hear the chiming of the bell and I do not expect to see another sunrise. If my legal adviser has been diligent, I will have received a direct cremation before you were apprised of my death and informed of your ongoing responsibility as sole executor. I apologise for not advising you of my decision in advance. I have my reasons which you will undoubtably discover in the fulness of time.

You will now possess an urn containing my ashes. I often spoke to you about the temple next to the Ashram I once stayed in - you know of it. It is my wish for you to deliver my ashes to be sprinkled over the river Ganges from the bank of the temple. The monks there will perform the appropriate rituals. While you are there you will meet an old friend of mine who I believe is still at the Ashram, for I would have known if he had died. He will help you in the search I feel in my heart you are about to embark on. It is my sincere wish for you to reside at the Ashram for a little while and listen closely to what he has to say - it will be our final lesson together and concerns the nature of truth.

I know you are a truth-seeker and I also believe you have the ability to be a truth-sayer - a person who instinctively feels the falsehood of the lie. And it is the lie I wish you to uncover within yourself. We have only disagreed over one matter - the issue of the symbol from which you created your company's now renowned psychometric assessment tool.

Your design was based on a series of mistruths concocted by someone who pretended to be something she was not. I am talking of the previous lady pastor at the Church of Universal Values. It is for you to determine the truth and rectify any damage which has been caused as a result of your work. The Pastor she replaced at the church is also an old friend of mine, though we do not communicate with each other as frequently as we did in the past. I would be very grateful if you could arrange to see him and inform him of my death. You know of the man as he was the Pastor of the church you attended with me during your holidays from The Boarding School.

He lives in the little village some 30 miles north of our city, you will find his contact details in my address book. He will aid you in the commencement of your journey. I should warn you has become somewhat cantankerous in his old age and may not take to you very kindly because of your role in developing the psychometric assessment. Nevertheless, he is a truth-sayer and he may well recognise the same talent in you.

Finally take a moment to look at the picture I have enclosed with this letter. In particular focus your attention at the centre of the cross. This was drawn and assembled some thirty years ago by four girls I was minding at the time. They each determined an individual element and we assembled them together to create the whole.

Their creativity was an inspirational reaction to a story I told them - one which you will also remember - the eating of the four fruits by the mother in the courtyard garden of Eden. The symbolism is obviously very old, archetypal, and each element would have been contained within their subconscious. In some traditions the symbol is known as Spiritualis Tabula Vitae Interiores. It is now time for you to determine the truth contained within the image.

Maybe we will meet again on another plane of existence. I must confess I know not what happens beyond the death of my mortal body. However, I have known for a long time that I am not my body - it has been merely my blessed home and temple for a short period of time on this earth.

May the love of our Lord's blessings be with you my dearest William

He places the letter back on the table and sits quietly reflecting on her words. He can taste their truth. The authenticity contained within them creates a sensation in his body of golden light, the light one would experience in the dawning of a fair summer morning. He picks up the picture and, as requested, looks closely at the centre of the cross. It takes a moment of time before he notices the small circle drawn into the paper. As he looks it appears to grow larger - moving from two dimensions into the third transforming itself into a perfectly round sphere. As he scrutinises the sphere it transforms into a multi-faceted emerald cut diamond sparkling in a non-existent sun, before returning to being a small, relatively insignificant circle in the centre of the cross.

Suddenly he feels tired. He looks around the room and decides to get up from the table and sit for a few moments in the old shabby Victoria winged back chair in a corner facing into the room.

It had been his favourite seat as a child and although very battered and worn with age it was, nevertheless, extremely comfortable. It had also been one of the Aunt's most prized possessions so when he was first allowed to sit upon it he had felt very privileged.

He sits down and leans back into the comfort of the chair as was his wont when he was a young boy, adopting the same habitual posture as he had so many years ago. He feels comforted and in a state of lost innocence - the innocence of his childhood. He closes his eyes momentarily and falls into a dream.

He is running down a straight path protected on each side by two large brick walls on which there is a vine growing. It is overcast, shadowy and uninviting. The line of the path and the walls have the appearance of stretching into eternity. There is no visible end in sight. He immediately recognises it as the path he drew at his office desk. He wants to escape so he turns around hoping to see the two pillars marking the entrance. There is no entrance - the line of the path is the same going backwards as it is going forward. He feels lonely, frightened, and lost. He wishes to escape – to wake up.

The old pendulum clock strikes five chimes and on hearing them his eyes instantaneously open. His attention rushes out into the light of the Aunt's living room. He shakes himself and without any conscious reasoning his body stands up out of the chair. He needs to be moving on - there is much to organise. He walks over to the table and picks up the letter together with the drawing and returns them carefully into the envelope. He places the envelope inside his jacket pocket. He picks up the urn and after turning to look at the clock one last time walks out of the living room, down the corridor and out through the front door.

Part 2 - The Chiming of the Bell

'The easing of pain lies within the ability to listen
for in solitude there is clarity.'

Many people are completely unaware of the time and hour when the slow chiming of the bell commenced within the individuality of their life. A lack of presence within the horizon of their soul could well explain their forgetfulness of being.

Do you remember when the bell first rang out for you? do you hear it even now?

Alas many no longer hear it. At an early age, whilst their progenitors continue to instil the habits of their own life upon them, most children lose their ability to sense the reality of the world surrounding them and cease to hear the relevance of the chiming bell in relation to their ongoing existence in this world.

We did not hear the very first chime of the bell as our infancy only came into fruition when our universal Mother placed her feet back down on the verdant soil upon which the tree she had ascended was nurtured.

She had partaken of the very fruit she had been expressly forbidden to eat - the golden fruit of knowledge, the silver fruit of creativity, the milk white fruit of service, and the olive black fruit of labour. It was through the lingering harmonics of the bell followed by a second chime when our universal Mother, now having partaken of the four fruits, realised the enormity of what she had set into being - for the ability to hear the chiming of the bell from which all creation was conceived represented the beginning of the human epoch.

This, of course, occurred many years ago within the inner courtyard of the garden of Eden, the place in which the tree of knowledge had been originally conceived and nurtured by the rather cantankerous gardener of those days. The controlling influence of the vine, also planted by the very same gardener, and within whose strong stems Eve had clambered up through the branches of the tree to eat the first fruit, was also within its unwieldy infancy; the Sign, the map on which all the events of the earthly world would evolve, was as yet undefined.

Yet since that time right up until this very day, at the commencement of each nativity, the birth is imbued in its sound and falls within the influence of the tolling bell.

The bell of your own lifeline chimes as we speak and whilst you may not be able to hear its toll, every second of your life plays out to its rhythm. Your reaction to the bell is unique (in as much as any one of you are truly distinctive from another) as you subconsciously become accustomed to the life it has created for you - for the rhythm of the bell is the rhythm in which the line of your existence is played out within the ebb and flow of your bodily functions.

Have a regard towards your friends - watch them closely - can you not see them reacting to the chimes of their existence?

You may choose to consider the chiming of the bell to be an insidious constraint placed upon your life - for at some inevitable point it will cease to chime for you. Whilst it will continue tolling for the others you leave behind, you will no longer share in their ongoing existence.

What happens after your death is something we have no cognisance of, for we are only the summation of your existence and the existence of everyone who came before you together with all those who will come after. We have no place beyond your sojourn within this realm.

So what is the truth of your life?

There are many who would claim to know the truth - they would say you have a destiny over and beyond the scope of the bell and its dismal toll. These people, who would profess somehow to know the truth, understand nothing of the subtlety of life as we have experienced it. Beware of these people, for there are many who constantly seek to make profit from their prophecies of doom. They hide in the caverns of worldly misery making their proclamations to those who are in desperate need to find an answer to the lack of direction they experience, and in their search to be saved will end up paying for the worthless falsehoods being peddled in their direction.

Your authentic friends are those persons who will help you find the truth but seek nothing in return for their assistance - for truth is not a commodity available to be purchased from others for a pecuniary benefit.

The Truth of your life on this earth can be heard within the chiming of the bell. If you listen to its sound it will reveal the path of destiny and the line of direction you need to take. The pain of your struggle lies within the ability to listen.

Chapter 3 - The Victim

'One person's truth
Is another's person's destruction.'

He awakes to find himself sat slumped upon a mock leather Chesterfield style chair in a large comfortable lounge surrounded by twenty or so other women and men - fellow residents of the All Care Private Country Nursing Home and Rehabilitation Centre. The room itself is well furnished with similar chairs and settees dotted around corporate style coffee tables on which there are placed an appropriate variety of books, magazines, and board games (mostly unread and unused). The illusion of quality generated is one replicated in the many exclusive retirement apartment complexes found increasingly for sale in the centre of towns and cities around the country.

Nevertheless, it is impossible not to recognise the room for what it is - the lounge of a nursing home catering for people suffering from various levels of incapacity. Most of the inmates are staring listlessly at a large screen television currently showing the iconic mid-morning chat show which is aired each weekday on national television. The volume is relatively low, however, if you are hard of hearing there is the induction loop which is always functioning effectively. The television is also programmed to display automated subtitles for the deaf - currently it is desperately trying to keep up with the pace of this morning's conversations. The residents who are not watching the television are fast asleep - as was the victim until a moment ago. The lounge is under the constant supervision of four carers - all registered nurses and suitably well remunerated for their work.

He looks around the room and is instantly confused - 'this isn't my home.' 'Is it time to go to the pub?' He turns over his wrist in order to check the time on his watch - but there is no watch there. Feeling increasingly disorientated he looks around at the other residents sitting in their chairs - 'which one am I married to?' He searches his pocket for his car keys and shouts out aloud to himself.

"Where the hell are my car keys? I need to go to the pub."

A carer from the other side of the room rushes over.

"Shush now. You'll upset the others."

"What others? Who? Where am I?" He peers at the carer trying to ascertain who she is. Certainly not a member of his team.

She takes his hand and presses it gently on his knee. "You are at home with us. We are looking after you."

"Where is my car and where are my keys?" He pauses. "I want to go and check in on my boat."

"Oh sweetie - you don't have a boat anymore - that was a long time ago. You are here with us now." She turns away as she hears someone groaning at the other side of the room. She removes her hand from his. "I will be back in a moment, behave yourself while I'm gone."

As she moves away he decides to stand up and embark on a search to locate his car. It will probably be in the car park. He stumbles and immediately falls back into his seat.

He glances around the room - it is full of old people. He doesn't understand what he is doing here. He is only 35 years old - he should be at work!

Ah yes, he remembers now. He is a senior manager of a leading professional service organisation. He has an important and responsible job. He is in the office surrounded by all these beautiful young women interns seeking to have sex with him in order to achieve promotion into the business. He doesn't blame them for he is notoriously good between the sheets in both an active and mutual way. He sees the young woman in the chair next to his looking at him with amorous eyes. He stands up, moves towards her, leans over and starts fondling her right breast.

"It's ok. I know what you are looking for and I will help you. You're new here aren't you? Let me show you the ropes."

He inclines his face toward hers and commences a slow lingering kiss on her lips. As his tongue enters her mouth he feels sudden pain as the object of his desire clenches her teeth around it. He pulls back and screams in pain. He looks at the young woman but she isn't there. Instead he sees an old crone who is laughing at him. He falls back into his chair.

"That'll teach you, you randy old bugger. I've dealt with the likes of you many times in my life and they were all much better looking than you."

The carer rushes over - she is slightly amused, the randy old bugger got what he deserved. She puts on her best severe face.

"Oh for god's sake you're not misbehaving again are you? Well, I will have to report this to the director. Your son's coming to see you later. Why do you have to be so naughty. Let me look at your tongue - go on open your mouth."

The victim opens his mouth and allows the nurse to look at his tongue. "Well, there's no damage done - you're not bleeding. Maybe you should go back to your room and rest so you're fit and ready to see your son when he arrives. I will get someone to help you." She calls over to a young male carer who has also been watching proceedings with a degree of some amusement from the other side of the room.

"Will you help this gentleman back to his room." The young carer acquiesces and walks over towards the victim.

"I don't need any help. I know exactly where I am." snaps the victim. He stands up slowly, stumbles slightly and automatically moves to the left towards the office door and corridor. Unfortunately the door for the communal lounge is on the right-hand side. He is bewildered.

"Where am I? I am not in my office." He pauses as he tries to come to terms with the truth of his current circumstance. He looks around the communal lounge and at the young man wearing a uniform. Of course, he concludes, he is being held in some sort of secure unit. How had he got here? He can't remember. He stumbles back into the chair.

He speaks slowly searching desperately for the appropriate words to convey the seriousness of his situation to the young man who is now standing over him and apparently offering to take his arm to help him get up out of the chair. "I understand what's going on, you have drugged me, no wonder I was confused. I am a prisoner and you are holding me against my will. My enemies have put me in here. Don't you know who I am boy?"

The carer smiles. "Of course I know who you are, I have read all about you in our medical files. Now let me help you back to your room."

The victim grimaces. "What do you mean you've read my files - they are classified - I am a one of the country's most senior politicians. You would do well to remember that my boy. Only last night I briefed the secretary general of the United Nations about this place and the experiments you are carrying out on the inmates in here. Everyone knows who I am. I will be rescued - mark my words. The country won't survive without me. Lead on - take me to my cell. I won't be there for long especially if my son is coming to see me. Then you'll really see who is in charge here and I wouldn't want to be in your shoes. You better know whose side you are on in the coming war - have you got that boy!?"

The male carer ignores the protestations, helps the victim up from his seat and leads him gently out of his chair, through the communal lounge door and up to his bedroom on the first floor. There he places him in a chair, pours him a glass of water, adds some thickener so he can drink it safely, places the glass on the side table and hands him the daily newspaper.

"I will come and look in on you in half an hour or so. In the meantime enjoy the paper and try to relax."

He walks out through the bedroom door and secures it.

****

He awakens on the chair in which he had fallen asleep two hours previously, stares around him, considers the half empty glass of water on the table, the paper open on his lap on a page commenting on the parlous economic state of the country and the government's presumed lack of ability to manage it.

With the god possessed clarity of his un-diminished intellect he suddenly recognises the truth of what is happening to him. He has been placed here out of sight and mind from a general public who now need him more than at any time previously. All of his generous and compassionate actions, his innocent opinions, his motivation to cure the world of all its ills, has led to this point.

He considers his current situation and with the realisation of his newly acquired self-knowledge concludes there is absolutely nothing he could of done differently to prevent this abhorrent abuse of power from taking place - he is faultless, there is no blame to attach to him or his behaviour of the past. He has become the victim of his own unfettered brilliance, misunderstood by all around him who have deserted him to face his victimhood in the isolation of this room in solitude. He has been incarcerated against his will by his political enemies.

He recalls what happened earlier in the day at the office - the young woman he had kissed. He is more than aware he is not perfect - no human being is - they all shit and procreate, even the so called messiahs. Yes - he has explored all the teaching and read the books - they were all so disappointingly lacking - lacking the truth which only he appears to see with alarming clarity. He knows the truth, he lives the truth, he speaks the truth, and yet no-one seems to recognise the truth when it is there to be seen within his own actions on a daily basis. His indisputable role in this world, he now realises, is to lead it to greatness.

He feels angry. Nevertheless, it does not pay to be angry in public unless the anger wears a smile. Yet having to live and work with people who are completely unable to see the world from his perspective is oddly trying and occasionally he will blow - like he did this morning in the office. He doesn't mean to - it's accidental, merely a by-product of the incredible challenging responsibility of being who he is. He is the one who has to wear his heart on his sleeve, who says it as it is. As President Truman once remarked: 'If you can't stand the heat get out of the kitchen'.

Unfortunately, he has not yet met anyone who is prepared to be burnt for the length of time it takes to purify their soul, especially the women.

Ahh, the women - all those women to whom he had given opportunities to share in his own special and rarefied world. He smiles as he remembers his erotic conquests - how many had subjected themselves to the stirring of his ever-greedy loins - it must have been over a thousand. He was not a selfish lover, they all claimed to have enjoyed him at the time. Yet on reflection each one had thrown away the gift he had shared with them.

He sighs in acknowledgement to the simple reality of how difficult it is to be him, especially now.

He is more than aware that many people feel themselves to be victims, but really? In the past some people even portrayed him as being the perpetrator of their own victimhood - especially the wives and girlfriends. They clearly misunderstood what it really means to be a victim - their asseverations only proved one thing - he is the victim, the victim of their ignorance - they did, by default, become the perpetrators of their own misfortune.

Whilst he acknowledges he will be judged on the culmination of his historic deeds, the reality of the past has to be interpreted the viewpoint of the present - this is how he understands without doubt what is essentially true. All actions viewed from now only have meaning in relation to his current existence, there is no need for any remorse on his part.

Yes, he sympathises with the psychological weakness of women - has he not recognised their fragility of both mind and body - he was their saviour. He had allowed so many into his bed. He had looked out for them while they chose to stay with him, given them a place, shared his intimate thoughts - if only they had listened to him and did as he said, everything would have been alright.

It is the peoples' inability to listen to the truth which construes the perennial problem. Arguably he is to blame for it is the by-product of his democratic nature. Everyone has the right to express their view and if the majority agree all is well. The issue is they frequently feel the need to propose courses of behaviour diametrically opposed to the greatness he is trying to achieve on behalf of everyone else.

He decides it must be time to go to the pub. He gets up from his chair and walks to door. He turns the handle but the door won't open to him. He pushes - no response. He looks for a lock but cannot see one. It is then he remembers - he is a prisoner - a prisoner of conscience. He has been incarcerated for his beliefs. He bangs on the door.

"Let me out of here! I demand to be set free. I need to see the governor at once. There has been a dreadful mistake. I shouldn't be in here."

He goes back to his chair, sits down, puts his head in his hands and sobs quietly.

There is a knock on the door and he hears the sound of a lock disengaging. He looks up as the door opens and two people walk in - both male. One turns to the other. "I will leave you with him. Any problems just press the call button on the wall near his chair and we will respond."

The other replies, "Oh I doubt there will be any problems - do you pops?"

The victim realises the person is addressing him - who is he? He considers the male in front of him and sees a tall, ruggedly handsome middle-aged man standing in front of the table looking down on him with a degree of amusement on his face. He notices immediately his visitor is expensively dressed in what must be a bespoke tailored single breast suit in a grey/blue weave and a monogrammed white Egyptian cotton shirt. He appears to be strangely familiar. He looks a little like him.

The other man gives the visitor a brief nod of acknowledgement, "I will catch up with you before you leave." He retires from the room and walks away down the corridor.

"Do I know you?" Asks the victim.

The visitor walks over to the other side of the room, picks up a chair, walks back and places it in front of the victim and sits down. He smiles at the victim with an unmistakeable hint of a condescension.

"Of course you do. I just called you pops didn't I. It is me, your ever dutiful and loving son. I have come to visit and see how you are doing."

"Ahh - I remember now. You have come to rescue me from my prison and return me to the heart of government where I belong." He stutters and peers at the visitor's face a little closer. "No, no, no. This will not do. You are the one who had me incarcerated in this prison. You usurped me! How dare you do this to me. You have no right. Get me out of here at once and I will treat you leniently."

The son chuckles - it appears to be a friendly laugh, yet it lacks any filial warmth. "Oh dear pops, you have got it so wrong. Don't you remember who you are and what you were. Yes, you were nearly successful once - evidently you managed to scale the dizzy heights of commerce and become a senior manager for a second-rate professional services organisation. You have never been a politician and with your past history - three divorces, the litany of discarded girlfriends and illicit lovers - it is unlikely any political party would have ever risked accepting you as a candidate.

"Whatever your fantasies are now, in reality you retired a sad and lonely little man of no consequence to anyone. Nevertheless, after the many years of our estrangement, I came back to your side and rescued you from the oblivion of retired life. We got on so amicably you gave me power of attorney and when you started to become incapable of looking after yourself both physically and mentally, I arranged for you to come here, a secure environment where you would be of no harm to yourself or anyone else.

"I don't want to be here." The victim replies sulkily.

The son walks over to the bay window and looks out over the expansive well-manicured gardens. "Oh come on pops. This is luxury. The best country house hotel you could choose to reside in. The residents are friendly. You get three good meals a day, and you are being well looked after. What more could you want?"

"I want to go to my boat. I want to make love to a beautiful woman and express myself fully as a man. I want to be recognised for who and what I am!"

The son regards the father "You are so ungrateful. Let us unpick each one of those last statements carefully and see if we can bring a little bit of reality to your current situation.

"Firstly, there is no boat, it was sold many years ago as part of your divorce settlement to my mother, your third wife if you remember. I know you liked to be called the sailor but in reality you never were - you never bothered to take the exam to qualify as a skipper. If you wanted to move the boat you had to hire someone else to do it for you.

"Secondly, the days when you could exercise your rampant libido on all and sundry has long gone by. In fact in today's working environments you would probably be sacked and taken to court for sexual misconduct - then you truly would be in prison. You are lucky no-one is trying to sue you for your past misdemeanours. I understand the residents here are infinitely less susceptible to your previously renowned charms. How is your tongue by the way - still hurting?

"Thirdly you are recognised for what you are - an old man suffering the infirmities of age and who needs the constant care and attention which I, your loving son, have arranged for you." He smiles beatifically towards his father inviting a response.

"You have usurped me." Growls the victim acerbically. "You would be nothing without me as your father. Come on tell me - where would you be now?"

"Exactly where I am at the moment, caring lovingly for my old pops. I seem to recall it was my stepfather who paid for my education (albeit with a reluctant contribution from yourself) and it was he who encouraged me in my studies at university. I believe it was my stepfather who advised me in my early career. And if I remember correctly you did not once prevail to provide me with any counsel. You were still too busy trying to propagate our species."

"And so I should. A person of my stature. You are the product of my loins. It is my intelligence coursing through your veins. Your mother was a simpleton - you got nothing from her. Of course you will never amount to much will you? The children of the wise seldom have the ability of their forebears. What say you? Now let's go to the pub and I will explain the error of your ways over a gin and tonic."

"I'm afraid we don't have time for a drink in the pub today. However, I will ask reception to bring us up a coffee if you want?"

"I don't want a coffee. I want to go home. As my son it is your duty to take me there at once if I should so demand. I am demanding."

"Oh pops, you certainly are. Don't you remember we sold your home to free up income so you could stay here. The money is running out and I have arranged to continue paying for you out of my own personal income. Fortunately I have enough to do so. I have spoken to the director of this establishment, and I am reliably informed you are not well enough to leave here without an equally expensive care package put in place wherever you reside. I am telling you this as a loving son. Unfortunately with my current responsibilities I do not have the resources to look after you in my own home, and there is no-one else I know of who would be prepared to do so."

"What about my wife, your mother. Where is she? Why hasn't she come to see me? She will look after me - I mean I have looked after her wellbeing for years."

"Come on pops - remember for god's sake. She divorced you after discovering you screwing her best friend in the marital bed on your tenth wedding anniversary. She is no longer your wife and with the best will in the world she is hardly likely to want to care for you after so many years."

"Divorced me did she! The ungrateful bitch. Just like all the others. They just never appreciated me. I always looked after their needs and they all threw me into the gutter. They betrayed me! Just like you are betraying me now. Don't you realise who I am."

The son smiles. "I just gave you the answer to that particular question. You are an old man suffering the infirmities of age and who needs the constant care and attention which I, your loving son, have arranged for you. Now I am sorry to say, I have got to go, important things to do and people to see."

The victim looks down at the paper and notices the article he was reading before he had fallen asleep. It was the commentary on the parlous economic state of the country and the government's presumed lack of ability to manage it. Now he fully understand the truth of what is happening in front of his very own eyes. Yes, he knows exactly who the person is sat in front of him claiming to be his son. Oh yes, he, the victim, has been placed out of sight and mind from the general public who need him now more than at any time previously. He growls and speaks from the clarity of his newly realised knowledge.

"I know who and what you are. You are no son of mine. And let me tell you if I was to stand against you in the particular beauty contest you are contriving to initiate I would win hands down. But I can't because you have imprisoned me here."

Before the son has a chance to reply there is a knock on the door and a young man enters.

"Sorry to bother you - the director asked me to look in to make sure everything is alright, and it is time to administer his afternoon medication. It won't take long."

The son tries not to look too relieved by this interruption. "Don't worry. I was about to leave anyway - things to do, people to see. I will leave you to it. Bye-bye pops. It has been lovely to see you. It may be a while before I can come again - but come again I will - rest assured. Look after yourself and don't go upsetting any more female residents." With these final words lingering in the air he stands up, smiles benignly at his father, and walks out through the door.

****

It is two hours later when he awakes on the chair in which he had fallen asleep, stares around him, considers the half empty glass of water on the table, the paper open on his lap on a page commenting on the parlous economic state of the country and the government's presumed lack of ability manage it, and realises immediately, with the god possessed clarity of his un-diminished intellect - he is the victim.

Chapter 4 - The Lady with the bag

'Beware of other peoples' assumptions
You may become lost within them.'

In the middle of the countryside, thirty miles north of a somewhat overpopulated city, there is a little market town in which resides an old coach house hotel - it is situated on the high street. The town itself is not unpleasant, yet neither is it particularly pleasing to the eye. It is rundown both economically and emotionally. In addition to the hotel the once vibrant high street currently proffers its townsfolk four charity shops, an undertaker, a newsagent cum post office, a small supermarket, a library, and a kebab house.

Although the countryside beyond the confines of the town's curtilage is relatively agreeable, it is not a location anyone would choose to visit voluntarily. Consequently, the hotel is the type of establishment where people generally book in for one night unless they have business in the area and are consigned by the limits of their company's expenses policy to take up residency within one of its economy priced bedrooms.

There are twenty-two such bedrooms, and some, allegedly, are ensuite. The brewery which owns the hotel likes to regard the establishment as being more of a watering hole than one providing accommodation and as such any ongoing maintenance is kept to the minimum - the last major renovations to the building were undertaken some thirty years ago. The premises are now as tired as the people it employs.

Whilst the brewery markets the hotel as a popular venue for the local punters to enjoy a cheap drink at any time during the day, on this particular weekday Wednesday lunchtime the saloon bar is only frequented by one patron, the lady with the bag, and the bartender who flitters between the saloon, the lounge and the reception area pretending to be busy.

The saloon bar, like the hotel itself, is fairly shabby without the chic. Although relatively small it is handsomely panelled in a dark and dirty brown oak. There is a small fireplace containing a single smouldering log in the corner facing towards the entrance, and an old juke box (no longer functioning) next to the wall opposite to the bar. There are four dark varnished veneered tables positioned along the wall also facing the bar. Each table enjoys the company of two threadbare upholstered seats with accompanying stools.

The lady with the bag is sat holding her half pint glass of bitter with the top of lemonade at a table to the side of the room away from the fire. The bag is sitting next to her chair on a stool.

She is a long-term resident of the hotel having already spent five nights in one of its single bedrooms. She has been booked in for fourteen days to provide a roof over her head whilst she tries to find somewhere new to live.

This luxury was bestowed upon her by her ex-landlords who have just evicted her from her lodgings - a single room and wash area in a converted garage next to the four-bedroom house they have just managed to sell. They have also furnished her with a little compensation as a sweetener to encourage her to vacate the premises without creating any problems for them and the prospective purchasers - there was no legal tenancy agreement in place, and she had lived there for over six and a half years.

She is relaxing with her drink in the saloon bar after a very busy and productive morning. She went to the library and was allowed to use a computer with internet access to search on-line for a new home. After several hours she has found a potential property in Ireland she may be able to afford with the small amount of compensation she has received - it will enable her to create a new life. For this is what she wants more than anything - the new beginning, preferably somewhere other than in this town - somewhere she will be taken seriously.

In her mind Ireland would be a perfect place to live – a place to be born again into a fresh world of hope with the blessings of peace and love. It will enable her to escape the mundane path her life has taken up until now. Enough is enough, she has always put everyone else's interests ahead of her own. She has been kind and giving - yet no-one seems to be prepared to take her seriously. It is time to look after herself for once - a time to become more dynamic - a time to reveal her truth to the world - a time to follow the path of her destiny.

The lady with the bag is enjoying her stay in the hotel - the tiny bedroom on the top floor of the building is simply opulent in comparison to the privations she has had to bear in her previous lodgings. She considers herself to be a clean and hygienic person who takes a certain degree of pride in her general presentation and the luxury of warm running water from a shower is something she has not experienced for some time.

Whilst she could never be considered as dirty or noxious in any way, she still manages to engender the impression of an old bookcase which hasn't been dusted for several years. Her apparel, whilst not being worn or tattered, is nondescript. She has long hair which she wears in a messy bun. It is not dyed yet radiates an unnaturally orange tint through the grey. This colouring developed slowly over the many years of a dedicated addiction to nicotine - an addiction she finally managed to relinquish some three years ago. Her figure would be classically described as round, with her bust larger than the rest of the body, narrow hips, and rather fuller midsection. However, with a body mass index of 24 her weight is just within what is medically considered appropriate for her height. She has a pleasant face and smiles frequently, especially at anyone who is prepared, or may be prepared, to learn about the special knowledge she possesses. Unfortunately, the smile reveals teeth which although appear clean have obviously suffered acutely from the aforesaid addiction to nicotine.

In her own eyes, and those of her family, she has never amounted to much and was never expected to. She blamed her parents for this. She was the second child, an unexpected gift from god when her parents were in their early forties. Her elder sister, some twenty years older, instantly took exception to her for disturbing the happy idyll she had previously enjoyed with her parents as the only child.

The elder sister, being deeply embarrassed by her parents' inability and stupidity not to take adequate precautions whilst undertaking an activity she could barely imagine them capable of, adopted a distant and disapproving inclination toward her younger sibling. As the years went by and the younger sister grew up, the elder sibling began to despise her even more and ridiculed anything she tried to achieve for herself, which, to be honest, was not very much.

Her parents doted on their unexpected bundle of heavenly joy, so consequently never really challenged her to do anything of any import. Having failed to achieve the prerequisite qualifications to gain a place at any third-rate university who may have been prepared to offer her one, the parents remained unduly unconcerned - "don't worry love," they said, "just find yourself a nice man to look after you. You deserve at least that much after all the pleasure you have brought us."

Well, that particular piece of advice had proved to be fruitless.

She dutifully found a handsome young man, married him, was divorced by the age of twenty-eight, lost the marital home, and returned childless to live with her parents and look after them throughout their ageing decrepitude.

Both parents had been diagnosed with several serious health conditions requiring constant care - diabetes, arrhythmia, and osteoarthritis. Whilst her return was supposed to be a short-term solution to provide the care needed, it ended up becoming a full-time role as her elder sister seemed to consider it to be her duty as the younger sibling to provide it.

Neither was the elder sister prepared to sanction any external care provision or move them into a care home - it would be too costly and negatively impact on the amount of any future inheritance they would both receive. There was to be no respite for the next seven years during which time her life stagnated, neither moving forward nor backwards.

The parents finally passed away in their late-seventies, one after the other in quick succession over a period of three weeks. She became homeless for the second time when her elder sister insisted she should vacate the property immediately so it could be sold to settle the estate.

The last will and testament was very clear - all the monies remaining from the estate (after taxes, duties and expenses had been remitted) would be divvied up equally between them. Nevertheless, for some reason she could never quite fathom out she received very little in the way of an inheritance. The possible explanation for this lay with her sister's husband.

Her sister was married to a relatively successful senior manager of a leading professional service organisation based in the city and she had arranged with her parents some years previously for him to become the sole executor appointed to administer their estate in the event of their death. Her logic was that it would be far cheaper for him to manage the legalities rather than employing a firm of solicitors to do it for them.

The younger sister never really trusted the husband - he appeared to have a roving eye and had made some rather inappropriate suggestions to her which she chose to ignore. She questioned the arrangements but was told by her parents not to bother her little head over such complicated arrangements.

Once probate was granted she challenged the sister over the amount of her inheritance. The sister was having none of it - she trusted her husband implicitly; he had incurred significant expenses which needed to be reimbursed. She made her position toward the younger sibling abundantly clear.

'I really don't know what you are complaining about - there's more than enough money to keep you sorted for life provided you look after it properly. Don't come running to me if you manage to squander it all away on one of your fanciful money-making ideas.'

Her sister had subsequently divorced the husband after discovering him expressing the full extent of his libido on top of her best friend in the marital bed. This had evidently transpired during the course of an afternoon party to celebrate their tenth wedding anniversary.

The younger sister had not been present at the time - anyway she would never have expected to be invited to attend such an important landmark event in the elder sibling's life.

Shortly afterwards the sister had met a wealthy landowner - a country gentleman. He asked her to marry him and she did, taking her two children from the previous marriage to live with her and her new husband on a large country estate. She adapted well to her new role, adopting all the airs and graces of a country lady as if she truly had been to the manor born.

Since then the elder sister has barely kept in touch with her - it is obviously beneath her station - though an occasional call will be received checking up on her. The younger sister has been instructed not to ring her unless, and only if, she is in any kind of trouble - there was after all the bond of familial history between them regardless of how regrettable and unfortunate it may have been.

The elder of her sister's children, the boy, has become some sort of politician, whilst the younger, a daughter, has married a bohemian writer. She had only ever met the children once many years ago when they were still quite young and before either of the sisters had divorced.

Following a little domestic disagreement with her husband concerning his latest lover, she had bestowed upon her elder sister and then husband the pleasure of a surprise visit - she needed somewhere to stay for the night and had even offered to sleep in her car on the driveway so as not inconvenience either of them. Her sister was none too pleased to see her and after a couple of hours she was asked to remove herself from the home, her car from the driveway, and never return unless invited - an event which has yet to materialise.

At the same time she also made it clear the younger sister was to have nothing to do with either the niece or nephew - she was a bad influence and there was to be no ongoing relationship - no birthday presents, no Christmas cards, nothing - and from that day forth there was indeed no contact between them.

There were insufficient resources from the inheritance to enable the purchase of a property she could call her own, so instead the money was slowly squandered away on the rent of a property she couldn't afford and various misguided attempts to start her own business - she had no desire to work for anyone else.

Following a ruinous attempt to establish a market stall selling polymer clay brooches she assembled from craft kits in her kitchen, she finally realised she had no alternative but to find some form of paid employment.

Regrettably, the absence of any meaningful qualification together with the simple fact she had never really had a proper job before proved to be a significant hindrance in acquiring one.

She was not sure what type of work she would like to undertake - she did not feel any inclination towards jobs in retail, catering, domestic cleaning, or manufacturing - she felt such work was beneath her. Finally, she successfully applied for and accepted a position as a personal care assistant.

She convinced her employers she had the requisite skills having looked after her parents. She started her new job immediately and was let go before the end of her probationary period - they seemed to think she was not appropriately suitable for the role. She then successfully applied for another care assistant role and was yet again released from employment before the end of the probationary period.

There was still a desperate need for money - so she began applying for any role advertised in the paper or posted in shop windows, including jobs in her previously proscribed despised list. She even registered with several recruitment agencies.

Regardless of her efforts no-one wanted to employ her - there was always someone more suitable -however, they would keep her details on their files just in case something popped out of the woodwork she was suitably qualified for. She never heard back from any of them.

As a result she became a permanent fixture at the local claimants centre whose personal job coaches/wellbeing advisers seemed totally incapable of assisting her in anyway other than by ignoring her existence and allowing her benefits to continue being paid in perpetuity.

The allowance provided was insufficient to cover her rent which was deemed excessive to her actual need. Consequently, she became homeless for the third time and moved into the barely habitable converted garage adjacent to the four bedroomed house from which she has now just agreed to be evicted from.

She has dutifully informed her sister of her current situation but knows better than to expect any kind of familial assistance.

Her lack of employment has given her ample opportunity for the contemplation of her predicament and the troubles facing many people like her.

She has researched and scrutinised the daily papers and other information she can glean from the local library. She has discussed her thoughts with likeminded people - people who like her are searching for an answer to their own personal life crises. She has now realised her own truth - she is wiser and more intelligent than most of the people around her. She has been granted a unique knowledge, setting her apart from her fellow humans. She knows what is going on in the world - the conspiracies ranging against her and her fellow travellers by the secret cabals who actually control life on earth.

Yet she now lives with the burden of an immense responsibility, for it is clearly her duty to share the unique knowledge she possesses with whomsoever will listen to her. Obviously, this does not include her sister who would never believe her and who has now become trapped by her new found wealth within the very system she requires protection from.

Nevertheless, the learning she provides almost certainly protects the listener and all those they love from inevitable destruction provided they are prepared to hearken to her words. Consequently it is incumbent upon her to engage with as many people as possible and explain to them the truth of their life and how they are under the control of an evil cabal who determine their behaviour do through lies and propaganda.

In order to achieve this particular objective her bag contains an assortment of gifts, complimentary sweets and chocolate bars, portions of crisps sorted into polythene bags, a collection of old magazines, several children's books, and some plastic toys. These goodies are refreshed every day during her perambulations around the neighbourhood and are always available to be proffered upon anyone who she may become friendly with, for she realises that when a person receives an unsolicited gift of obvious thoughtfulness they will be more inclined to pay attention and concentrate carefully on what she has to tell them.

This lunchtime she has already endeavoured to engage with the bartender who had just served her the half pint of bitter with a top of lemonade. She hadn't met him before so presented him with a portion of crisps and a pineapple chew by way of introduction.

Unfortunately, before she had chance to educate him in the ways of her special knowledge he had excused himself in order to take a comfort break. It was particularly fortunate for the bartender that she didn't see him assigning the possession of her priceless gifts to the waste bin residing between saloon bar and lounge bar.

She is now sat poised, ready and waiting for the bartender to return or to pounce on any other unfortunate customer who happens to enter.

She relaxes for a moment and takes another slow draw from her half pint glass of bitter with the top of lemonade and removes a portion of crisps from her bag along with the papers she printed off at the library earlier. She opens the freezer bag containing the crisps and begins to eat them as she looks dreamily at the pictures of the property she is determined to buy. Her eyes become misty as she imagines herself living within this idyll.

She jolted out of her daydream when she hears the bartender addressing a customer. She hadn't noticed him returning from his comfort break. Neither had she registered the customer entering the saloon. She looks to see who it is expecting it to be one of the regular lunchtime crew. No, she has never seen this man before.

Instantly this new customer becomes a person of interest to her, someone she can engage with and possibly share her unique knowledge of the world with. She studies him closely - the man is of smart appearance, clean, well dressed with a taste for expensive casual clothing. He is neither ugly nor good looking though relatively tall, trim - probably an accountant.

She looks on as he purchases a bottle of Italian beer. Yes, this is someone she should engage with, someone she can pass on her knowledge to. She feels excited, ultimately saving this person will make her afternoon a great deal more pleasurable than she was expecting it to be.

She stares at him with the intention of making him turn around and look at her. Some would argue this is an extremely rude thing to do, nevertheless, she has found on numerous occasions that such a fixed look generally achieves her objective. Sure enough he instinctively feels her gaze upon him, turns around and catches her eyes looking within his own. He seems momentarily confused - wondering who this woman is. Nevertheless, he smiles.

"Hello, do I know you?"

"You look like an accountant, are you an accountant?"

"No, I'm not an accountant," he laughs quietly as if to himself, "however, I do know quite a few. They are quite useful people occasionally, nevertheless, it was never a career I was particularly interested in pursuing." He pauses and waits for her response.

She remains staring at him fixedly before continuing.

"There's something about you - you must be an auditor or a financial adviser. Help me out here - you're not the usual customer we get in this bar - for a start you spoke to me. Most people around here ignore me. Come and sit down for a moment. I want to talk to you. Don't be scared. You can have a crisp." She moves her bag from off the stool and points at it indicating this is the place where he should sit.

The customer turns away for a moment and takes a mouthful of beer from his bottle. He looks around the room appearing to try and find someone to rescue him. There is no-one but the two of them - the bartender has returned to the lounge.

The woman with the bag scrutinises him carefully – looking for the tell-tale signs by which she will know beyond doubt he is a vessel fit to receive her learning. At the moment he appears to be well and truly outside of his comfort zone, as if in fact the hotel was really not the sort of place he was used to frequenting, and she was not the type of woman he was used to associating with. She addresses him again.

"Come on, there is only me and you here. I won't hurt you. We may as well have a little conversation to help the afternoon on its way. I haven't spoken to anyone all day except the bartender, and he can only grunt." She continues to stare at the customer.

He seems to be struggling over whether or not to join her. Finally a decision is made - he moves away from his position at the bar and walks slowly towards her table. He stands above the stool for a moment as if reaffirming the veracity of the decision he has made, moves the stool slightly away from the table and sits down. He does appear to be a little reluctant to get too close to her.

"There you go. That wasn't too difficult. Now tell me - you must be a lawyer."

He smiles - rather ruefully she thinks.

"No, I'm not a lawyer either though I know quite a few of them as well." He pauses for a moment as if trying to work out who or what he is before continuing, "I'm actually not from around here. I'm taking a sabbatical from my career - so I guess I'm not really anything at the moment other than a customer in a hotel bar. Anyway, I'm here to meet an old friend of my Aunt who died recently and I need to speak to him about her. I will sit with you until he arrives." He pauses for a moment and is relieved to see she has stopped staring at him quite so intently.

"So seeing as you are so interested about what I do - tell me about yourself, what do you do for a living? Are you an accountant?" He smiles towards the lady with the bag.

Quick as a flash she replies as if expecting the question.

"Actually, I'm the best-selling author of a book I haven't written yet. It's called 'how to eat a sausage and never get fat.'"

The customer laughs for a moment before realising she is being deadly serious. He stops his laughter and looks at her thoughtfully - her whole demeanour portrays an impression of melancholic loneliness.

She remains silent for a moment apparently upset by his response.

The customer, being unsure of how to assuage the situation he has accidently instigated through his thoughtless laughter asks, "have you had a bad day by any chance?"

She peers thoughtfully down at the papers printed off from the library earlier which are now positioned next to her half pint glass of bitter with the top of lemonade before looking up at him again.

"No worse than normal when you find yourself homeless for the fourth time in your life and stuck in a hotel like this wondering what to do next. Especially difficult if you weren't expecting your life to turn out this way. Not that I really expected anything special from life - just what everyone else had - a marriage, children, work, feeding a husband, having loads of sex, drinking wine under the moon, gazing into my lover's face behind the warm glow of a candle, being happy - was that too much to ask for?"

"Did you find any of it?"

"I found a husband - I loved him and gave him everything until he found a new model to play with. The generous sod wanted to share her with me. He couldn't understand why I didn't. He's long gone now."

"Children?"

"No, he didn't want to share me with children." She picks up her glass of bitter with a top of lemonade and takes the tiniest of sips. She scrutinises the customer's face.

"What colour are your eyes?" she inquires suddenly. "It says a great deal about where you come from - the colour of your eyes. Dark eyes you are born for the sun - light eyes you are born for the moon. Look I have light eyes, I am born for the moon."

He examines her face but cannot determine what the colour of her eyes actually are. He is lost for words and a silence pervades the conversation. The lady with the bag notices and recognising silence makes people feel uncomfortable decides not to allow the moment to remain unrequited. She picks up the papers from the table, shuffles them around and selects one sheet.

"I'm looking for a house." she says proudly as she passes him over a picture of a rundown one-bedroom shack in Ireland. "See how cheap it is. It's so cheap in Ireland. I can afford to buy it. It doesn't have a toilet or bathroom, but you don't need either if you can go and swim in the sea every day."

She pauses for a moment and undertakes a critical survey of the man opposite. Liking what she sees she continues.

"I think I used to like sex, or at least the imagination of it. What about you. Are you into it?"

"I'm celibate."

She laughs out aloud. "So you must be a catholic priest out of uniform. I bet you masturbate often enough though. Closet gay perhaps? Most of you are, I've read all about it. Do you have a big penis?"

"What?"

"Well the bigger the prick the smaller the brain. Most priests are big dicks. Everyone knows that."

He laughs in reply. "I am certainly not a priest. I've just never found anyone to share my life with on a personal basis. Sex never really interested me either, I know it does for the majority. I was engaged to my career. I never had the time for a relationship and it never really crossed my mind that I needed one. However, the reason I am taking a sabbatical is so I can gain a fresh perspective on life, especially after the death of my aunt. I need to rediscover a sense of purpose, find myself, and understand the truth of my life."

Silence. So, he does wants to know the truth about his life? This was the sign she was looking for. Well now, she knows the truth, should she tell him? It's complicated - the truth always is. Yet here he is, a person readily seeking the truth and looking to be saved. She can provide him with everything he needs in order to be rescued. She feels a pulse of excitement flurry through her body - a dizzy feeling in her head - a blurring in the eyes.

She loses attention and momentarily forgets where she is. She looks around feeling increasingly confused. She notices that the smouldering log in the fireplace has finally ignited fully into flame and decides to move herself and the bag from the table to the one closer to the comforting warmth it is now emitting.

She stands up abruptly and walks across the room and settles herself down on the chair next to the table by the fire, places the bag on an adjacent stool, and plonks the file of papers in front of her.

She looks around and sees the customer watching her quizzically with a certain degree of concern on his face. She immediately recalls where she is and what she has just said about masturbation and priests and frets she may have appeared rude - she would never want anyone to consider her as being discourteous, especially if they, like her, were searching for the truth. She calls over to him.

"Come and join me by the fire if you would like - I didn't mean what I said. I was just feeling a little cold. Anyway there's something I need to tell you, especially if you are truly searching for the truth. I have the answers you are looking for."

The customer smiles politely but remains in his seat. "I am all ears. What do you need to tell me? I am listening."

She looks at him with a puzzled expression - why hasn't he moved away from his seat? Surely if he realised she was about to reveal the secrets she had managed to discern through her own diligent research - secrets only she was cognisant to - he would have joined her by the fire. Was he truly ready to hear what she had to tell him? She wasn't so sure now. Would he actually take what she had to say seriously?

She examines his face again carefully searching for the signs that would reveal whether or not she should trust him...

Well, he looks sympathetic, considerate, and intelligent enough to recognise the honesty of what she is about to explain to him.

She decides she will give it a go - he will either be saved or lost, it is up to him. Her eyes shine with the excitement and knowing of a person ready to tell a confidence no-one else has heard before.

"It's all happening outside." she speaks quietly, conspiratorially.

"What is?" inquires the customer.

"The quickening. It's finally accelerating after all these long years of awaiting."

"I am not sure I know what you are talking about." the customer responds.

"The quickening - for god's sake - can you not experience it? You know - it's what all us truth-seekers have been talking about for years and now we are witnessing the happening in our lifetime - the end of all the lies and the beginning of truth!"

"I am really not sure I understand what you are speaking about." The customer speaks with a quiet and calm voice as he sees the look of exasperation growing on the face of the lady with the bag.

"Oh come on you do! Stop pretending. You've just told me you are searching for the truth. The plot has been discovered and we have lived within the lie for so many years. The quickening has finally accelerated and we no longer have to live the corporate lies. They have been polluting our drinking water with special chemicals to keep us under control. All those airplanes in the sky pretending to take people on holidays spraying the same chemicals into the atmosphere in order to change the way people think. This doesn't include you or me as we are immune to the lies we are being fed. We are seekers of the truth. History is a lie - created by the people in servitude to Satan and the Pope - he has six wives and three concubines, all who have produced three triplets. This proves it all - three to the power of nine. The corporate sign is the roman symbol for one thousand. Divide this by the three points on top and multiply by the two points below gives you 666 - the sign of the antichrist. The corporate world has taken us over and the acceleration of the quickening is the truth revealed to all who are prepared to be rescued."

She stops momentarily and regards the customer cautiously. He has obviously not understood a word she has been talking about. The customer looks back at her not sure what he should say. Her face relaxes - she smiles. He feels a sense of relief from the intensity of her conversation.

"Of course," she says, "I see it now. You really don't understand. This is the difference between us. I am being honest with you and yet you cannot see the truth when it is revealed. Would you consider yourself to be an honest or a truthful man?"

"Honest? I would certainly like to be considered as a truthful man. Is there a difference?"

"I like the truth - however it manifests. It comforts and upsets me. Nevertheless, it allows me to see things for what they truly are. As I have been trying to explain to you."

"Isn't that honesty?"

"Of course not - honesty has nothing to do with reality. Honesty is purely the ability to reveal what you feel. Is what you feel the truth? I doubt it very much. Are you an honest person or a truthful person? And how would you know?"

The lady with the bag suddenly realises they are no longer alone - the old man with the cassock has just walked in and is staring rudely at her. He always appears at the same time every day for a half pint of stout. She had had a fruitless conversation with him just the other day. For all his supposed knowledge he knew nothing - and when she tried to share her truth with him he had been offhand, offensive and rude. Nevertheless, she smiles at him sweetly, and he growls in return as he notices the customer sat at the opposite side of the room to her.

The lady with the bag returns her attention to the customer and smiles. "Ask him over there about honesty and truth, he's a vicar. Or at least he used to be one before they defrocked him." She turns to the old man in the cassock. "Yes, I've done my research on you - especially after our last conversation. I know all about you."

The old man in the cassock glares at the lady with the bag and retorts thunderously, "If you had done your research properly you would realise I was not defrocked but retired against my will." He turns to the customer and addresses him directly without lowering the tone of his voice ensuring the lady with the bag hears everything he is about to say.

"Well I guess you must be the chairman of RLE Services PLC. I bet she doesn't realise who you are or I doubt she would be speaking to you. In her eyes successful business people like you, and corporate companies such as yours, are the spawn of Satan committed to the destruction of the planet. Has she been filling your time with her useless baggage of conspiracy flavoured crisps. Buy her a drink. It will keep her happy. Then we will go and have our conversation in the privacy of the lounge bar." He returns his glare upon the lady with the bag

The lady with the bag downs the remainder of her half pint glass of bitter with the top of lemonade and places the empty glass on the table. She waits until the customer gets up and walks over to her table and picks up the glass to return it to the bar. She gazes at him impassively.

"I should have guessed you were one of them - it's why you look different. I can't say it's been a pleasure meeting you - you knew exactly what I was talking about. I will have a drink though, it's the least you can do - an apology for not being honest and telling the truth. Look closely at yourself and you will discover you are part of the problem. Maybe in time you will come to learn the error of your ways. Most likely you are beyond being saved - the quickening will finish you off together with all your corporate capitalist comrades and the heretics like him."

She turns away, picks up the pieces of paper she has printed off from the library and pretends to scrutinise them closely whilst the old man with the cassock and the customer leave the saloon bar for the lounge.

Being so deep within her own thoughts she barely acknowledges the bartender when he places the half pint glass of bitter with a top of lemonade in front of her.

She picks up the glass and takes a long slow sip of the cold liquid before placing it back on the table. Feeling the radiant heat of the fire warming her body she falls gently into a daydream about her new home, the desolate beaches she will discover, and the freedom she will find there. The daydream becomes a slumber and her head falls downwards into her chest. The bartender notices she has fallen asleep but chooses not to awaken her, leaving her on her own in the corner of the bar, close to the fire, whilst he returns to reception. She snores gently.

About an hour later, she wakes up with a start. There is a voice addressing her.

"Hello aunt."

She looks up in surprise and pretends not to have been asleep. She sees a tall, ruggedly handsome man standing in front of the table and looking down at her. She notices immediately he is expensively dressed in what must be a bespoke tailored single breast suit in a grey/blue weave and a monogrammed white Egyptian cotton shirt.

"Hello, do I know you...?" She asks.

"Of course you do - didn't I just call you aunt? Don't you recognise me? Say hello to your loving nephew." He smiles.

She looks at him carefully. She can see a family resemblance. She does recognise him, but not as her nephew. The man standing above her is often to be seen on the daily news and appears regularly as a guest on the internationally renowned mid-morning chat show aired each weekday on national television. She has also regularly read about him in the daily tabloid newspapers.

She had never realised this man was her nephew. She feels irritated.

"So just exactly how am I supposed to know you are my nephew? Obviously I can put a name to you. You're the poncey politician who's always on the telly spouting out spurious nonsense and pretending to be so knowledgeable about nothing and everything. I had no idea you were my nephew, and frankly it wouldn't have made any difference to my life if I had known. Politics doesn't really interest me - I am only interested in the truth - the real truth. Politicians are only interested in themselves, generally on the take, always corrupt, and never truthful." She glares at him demanding a response.

The nephew appears non-plussed for a moment. He had assumed his aunt would know who he was. Well never mind it wouldn't take him long to get her eating out if his hand, in a manner of speaking. He predicates what he has to say with a humorous laugh.

"Surely dear aunt you recognised my surname at least."

She continues to glare at him. She is confused. Why is he here? What does he want with her. The sister had made it so plain all those years ago - she was to have nothing to do with her nephew or niece.

"I haven't a clue what my nephew's surname is. Your mother divorced your father years ago. Re-married and neglected to invite me. She ordered me to have nothing to do with either my nephew or niece. I am about as interested in you as your mother is interested in me."

Well my darling aunt. It is a good job she is more interested in you than you realise. She let me know of your little predicament and has asked me to help you out - so here I am. Rest assured, you really do have a family who is prepared to love and care for you. This is why I have arranged for you to go and stay at a little residential home I know of for a few days. Whilst you are there we can give you a medical check and make sure you are fully fit and healthy after all of your unfortunate recent travails. Then we will help you decide where the best place for you to live - preferably somewhere you will never again be made homeless."

She picks up the sheaf of papers from the table containing the details for the property in Ireland and hands them to the nephew.

"This is where I want to live - arrange it for me." She places a determined look upon her face.

The nephew picks up the sheaf of papers, looks through them and bursts into laughter.

"Oh my dear aunt - you cannot be serious..." He continues laughing, "I think we can do better than this little hovel."

She feels a shiver go through her body. Something is not right. She sees a man walk into the bar. He is extremely tall, fit, muscular, bearing a demeanour very similar to a professional night club bouncer. He walks up to her nephew.

"Ok sir, I have got her belongings. There isn't very much. I have put them in the car. We are ready to go."

The nephew gazes at the aunt with a look she identifies as being one of total condescension.

"You need to come along with me aunty. It's time to come home to the welcoming bosom of your loving family. We only want to help you. My friend here will walk you to the car..."

Fifteen minutes later they arrive at the gates of an old country manor house. The muscular man gets out of the car and presses an intercom. The gates swing open and the man returns to the car, gets back into the driver's seat and motors slowly up the driveway towards the house where there appears to be a welcoming committee anticipating their arrival.

There is a man in the centre of the group dressed in a smart suit - she likes the look of him. Then there appears to be some stern looking women and a young man dressed in uniforms not dissimilar to the one professional nurses would wear.

She turns to the nephew. "What am I doing here. Who are they?"

"Nothing to worry about. Treat this as a holiday in an upmarket country house hotel - it's so much better than the one you had checked into. These people are here to look after you and ascertain your needs. They are really friendly. And don't worry about the cost of staying here, I am covering it for you."

He opens his door and gets out. Then opens the rear passenger door for the aunt.

Come on now aunt, let's go and introduce you to them - they are expecting you, and they are certainly looking forward to meeting you. I promise."

Chapter 5 - The Pastor (who was retired)

'A truth expounded as such becomes the lie.
Eventually the lie becomes the truth
for within the belief of one is the conception of the other.'

The habits some people acquire in life will never change - primarily because the person does not recognise that their daily behaviour is habitual. The way they walk, the way they talk and interact with others, the little things they do each day to give their life some structure and meaning. These habits become such an essential feature of their life that in their absence the person would simply cease to exist.

The Pastor of this story is one such person, though if you were ever to challenge him on the matter he would argue his habits were much more than the mundane reactions to daily living - they were in fact rituals bringing him closer to the source of all being.

It was just over nine years ago when the Pastor was unceremoniously removed from his post as minister of the Church of Universal Values - an independent church of no official denomination located in the outskirts of the somewhat overpopulated city. He was retired against his will to make way for a young female substitute who had been identified as an individual infinitely more qualified than he to superintend the church toward a new era of modernity.

His highly esteemed successor subsequently failed to achieve any of the performance targets set out for her, was unable to rebrand the church to attract a more diverse congregation, was found lacking in the duty of care toward her flock and preached a doctrine which was considered to be of a distinctly dubious origin, and one which certainly did not concur with the church's supposed line of esoteric thought.

She remained within her role as pastor to the congregation for less than two years - a significantly shorter period than the twenty-three years during which he held residency. She absconded from her duties shortly after the current tranche of church elders realised that in addition to the deficiencies in her abilities they had already identified, she was also in possession of a fairly significant drink and drug habit.

She vacated the manse on the very morning they were due to fire her from her position - the previous evening they had discovered her in the church unconscious in the possession of several empty bottles of Bourgogne and had vomited onto her lap whilst simultaneously urinating (not intentionally of course) all over the pew she was sitting on.

Several weeks thereafter the church elders were not particularly amused to further discover she had sequestrated the fees they had agreed with RLE Incorporated Limited for undertaking a little research on their behalf.

The company wanted the church to advise them on the origins and provenance of the sign they were using as their company logo - they understood the image was a direct copy of the cross hanging above the church's altar.

The church elders gave the girl minister the opportunity to undertake the research - it was considered she might gain a greater appreciation of the church's traditions from spending a little time studying the archives.

The elders had been intrigued to learn that the design of their rather unique cross was being used as the business logo for the company and had been utilised as such since the company's inception - in fact, if they themselves had taken a little time to reflect upon the church archives they would have realised it had been purloined for such use many years beforehand by a young couple who had been active members of the congregation.

He had been the pastor at that time and had considered their appropriation with the then church diaconate. The upshot of their consideration was that whilst the design of the cross was indeed peculiar to the church, its symbolism had a universal provenance having existed in similar forms within the many different religions of the world since time immemorial - it was, in fact, a representation of the Spiritualis Tabula Vitae Interiores. Therefore, there was no copyright, neither was it a registered trademark - the sign was technically held within the public domain and as such there was no legal recourse available to the church to prevent its use by the couple.

The diaconate also assumed the couple possessed neither the comprehension of, nor the ability to ascertain, the unique significance of the esoteric knowledge concealed within the symbol, therefore, what possible harm would occur through its utilisation as a logo for their rather silly and immature pseudo psycho-spiritual business - the Religion of Least Effort (RLE™)? It would soon fall out of use and be quietly forgotten about when their business eventually failed and collapsed - which it most obviously would. How wrong they had been...

After peddling their peculiar beliefs over a number of years, the couple died tragically in a plane crash over the rain forest of Borneo. Under the management supervision of the guardian of their one and only son, The Religion of Least Effort (RLE™) was transformed into a lucrative global professional services organisation specialising in health, wellbeing and wellness in the workplace through the provision of learning, development, training, and human resources.

The company, having now been rebranded as RLE Incorporated Limited, was handed over to the stewardship of their son and it was at his request the company's Director of Business Development approached the church to discover more about the origins of the image they were still using as their company logo.

After the elders had given their blessing to the girl minister to undertake the research on their behalf, she proceeded to concoct some flight of fancy from the few historical records she had bothered to glance through. She achieved this feat, as he was later led to believe, on the very same day she was discovered drunk as a skunk in the church.

When she realised she was most probably going to be dismissed from her role (she had been ordered to pass the keys of the church over to the treasurer and secretary who had found her, and forbidden to re-enter the building until they had decided upon her ongoing future) she immediately arranged to meet the Director of Business Development the following morning in a local coffee shop, where she seduced him with her womanly wiles, and promptly sold her so called research directly to the company behind the backs of her former employers.

From this intelligence of dubious origin they somehow managed to cobble together a psychometric assessment profiling tool which purported to enable anyone to easily comprehend their personal preferences for life and work, and determine the necessary actions needed to be taken in order achieve inner self-contentment.

Several years later the company merged with ROC Services PLC and is today known as RLE Services PLC. The chairman of what has now become a large internationally renowned conglomerate is none other than the son who originally inherited the parent's business all those years ago. Not only is the original logo still used as the brand image through which the RLE Services PLC is marketed, its outline is used as the framework onto which the psychological preferences of an individual are mapped.

Over the years since its accouchement from the total balderdash provided by his successor, the psychometric assessment has become the government's preferred model for the engagement of employees within the public sector. As a result it has also gained an increasingly positive reputation internationally and is currently utilised for all sorts of weird and wonderful purposes throughout the world of industry and commerce, leadership development, and recruitment. It is relatively fair to say none of these purposes bear any particular relationship to the esoteric truth represented within the symbol on which it was based - the Spiritualis Tabula Vitae Interiores.

When he first learnt that a psychometric assessment tool had been developed from the Spiritualis Tabula Vitae Interiores, he was outraged and entered into a rather heated exchange of correspondence with the then company secretary and head of legal services at RLE Incorporated Limited - but it was all to no avail. He was even threatened with legal action for defamation if he continued to cast negative aspersions over the research the company had undertaken in developing their model.

The company secretary and head of legal services has now transmogrified through promotion to become the chief executive of RLE Services PLC, and he has heard through the village grapevine the self-same man has moved into a cottage on the very same lane where he lives.

A neighbourly visit will most certainly be warranted in due course to introduce himself in person and 'welcome' him to the local neighbourhood. To say he still deeply resents how the symbol has been purloined and used to beget a substantial income stream for RLE Services PLC would be an understatement, and whilst he appreciates anger is detrimental to the development of the soul, he believes his version to be more akin to righteous indignation.

Shortly after his successor had been fired he was visited by a committee of the church elders, which still included within its number some of the members who had originally determined his retirement. They prayerfully requested he should see fit to gracefully return and lead the congregation in accordance with the original doctrinal canon of the church.

In recompense he would be allowed to live out his remaining years in the manse and take sole responsibility for finding the suitable apprentice who would eventually succeed him when he died - for indeed none of his predecessors had ever been asked to retire and had continued ministering unto the faithful members of the church until their natural expiration from the mortal plane of humanity.

He refused their prayerful benediction and referred them to the text of his final sermon - there would be no going back, he was the last in the line of pastors who had followed a tradition established by the church's founder. This tradition was transmitted orally from one pastor to the next over a significant apprenticeship. When he left that tradition was ended - he had no desire to return.

His act of demurral should not be considered as a form of retribution for what the church elders had inflicted upon him, though the words from St Paul's letter to the Galatians Chapter 6 verse 7 - 'for whatsoever one sows, that shall he also reap...' resounded through his mind. Quite simply, although he had not appreciated the concept of retirement at the time of his dismissal, he has now discovered the additional hours he has during the day for prayer, meditation, growing vegetables, and a half pint of stout in the local old coach house hotel, are particularly pleasurable.

His habitual routine commences every morning at 6.00 am when he arouses from his slumber. There is no need for an alarm for it is only very rarely will he awaken before or beyond this particular hour of the day - obviously there is the occasional confusion, generally twice a year when the spring shoots forwards and the autumn falls back.

He vacates his single dormitory style bed, goes to his bathroom, washes, shaves, dresses into one of his old black threadbare cassocks, and proceeds to the kitchen where he will place an old iron kettle upon the stove, wait for it to boil, place some leaf tea in an old enamelled tea pot, pour the boiling water from the kettle over the leaves, allow for it to brew before decanting it into a large old battered white porcelain mug (which happens to be nearly as old as he is) with a little drop of goat's milk.

By 6.30am he will go to the little chapel he has fashioned for himself in the spare bedroom, put on his surplice, light a votive candle on his altar under the picture of Madonna and child, sit on one of the three pews he managed to rescue from an antique warehouse, find sensation in his feet, close his eyes, and begin to recite his Kyrie Eleison. He will continue his meditation for forty-five minutes exactly when he will, without any obvious prompting, stand up, make the trinitarian sign of the cross whilst reciting his favourite personal prayer - *'dear lord let the light of your love shine through my heart in all my dealings with the world today.'*

He will return to his kitchen, brew another large mug of tea mixed with a little goat's milk and eat a small bowl of muesli, which he prepares the night before mixing it with a little sheep's yoghurt and stewed fruit. After breakfast he will go for a short bicycle ride around the village lanes and occasionally stop to converse with his neighbours.

He will arrive back home at around 10.00am and complete whatever chores he has listed out for himself to do the night before - these will generally involve undertaking a little bit of cleaning around the bungalow and doing his laundry. At 1.30pm he will ride his bicycle into the small market town bordering onto his village where he will enter the old coach house hotel and order his half pint of stout. There he will sit at the corner of the bar and drink it, unless it is particularly busy, in which case he will remove himself to the quiet solitude of the lounge.

He will then return home, go into the garden and complete the tasks required to keep his little plot of land bountiful and beautiful in the eyes of god. After a couple of hours of diligent labour he will harvest whatever vegetables are in season - these he will then prepare for his supper. His diet is primarily vegetarian although he allows himself the luxury of a little goats milk, butter and cheese. What he eats is therefore dictated by what nature determines can be safely gathered in.

He takes the preparation of his food seriously with intention towards the process. When he cleans and chops his vegetables he endeavours to remain conscious of what he is doing. Likewise, when he eats he prefers to consume his food not his thoughts. Whenever he observes his mind wandering he stops eating, puts the knife and fork on his plate and rededicates his food to god through a simple act of prayer.

After supper he will retire and devote himself to a little reading or some writing (he keeps a daily journal) before returning to the chapel for his evening devotional meditation. he will recite his personal liturgy for Compline which he has adapted from the book of common prayer.

Before the conclusion of his day, he will return to the kitchen, compose the list of the chores which need to be undertaken the following day and pin it onto his notice board next to the fridge, prepare his muesli with the yoghurt and stewed fruit, place it into the fridge, and finally retire to his bed.

On this particular morning he awakens as usual at 6.00am and immediately proceeds with the habitual daily routine. However, as he arises out of his bed he remembers that today is going to be slightly different from the norm - he has agreed to meet someone at the old coach house hotel for a drink -

the chairman of RLE Services PLC no less - 'for whatsoever one sows, that shall he also reap...'

It is finally harvest time, metaphorically speaking of course, and he has a scythe to sharpen for he intends to show the man the parlous state of his crops. Not that the chairman is aware of this fact yet - he has arranged to meet with the Pastor to discuss the death and funeral arrangements of an old member of his church - a person he had himself been particularly fond of.

She had died recently and for some reason he can't quite fathom out yet, the chairman is her sole heir and executor. In the meantime his proposed visitation upon the chief executive to welcome him to the neighbourhood can be postponed - the chairman is a much larger fish to fry and dealing with the person he considers most culpable for purloining the Spiritualis Tabula Vitae Interiores will be infinitely more pleasurable.

He arrives at the hotel at exactly 2.00pm, chains his bicycle in the courtyard and enters the lounge through the back door. He walks through the lounge into the bar, takes a moment to look around, and immediately perceives a customer who is most probably the chairman of RLE Services PLC.

The chairman is immaculately dressed with an obvious taste for expensive casual clothing. He looks rather uncomfortable. He is being blethered at by the crazy lady with the bag - a temporary resident of the hotel. He had the dubious pleasure of an audience with her the previous day during which she had endeavoured to engage him with her banal conspiracy theories.

She notices him and has the audacity to smile in greeting. He really has no time for people like her - he has never considered it to be his duty to repair those who are broken, it is not within his calling. No, his role as a pastor was to be an educator to the converted and help those who turned to him for guidance to find mystical union with the universal source of everything - for truth is a limited commodity and there is not enough of it to feed everyone. Not all are chosen to be saved and it was never his job to convert atheists or people who believe in utter garbage like her. He grimaces in response to her smile.

The lady with the bag continues with her prattle toward the customer. "Ask him over there about honesty and truth, he's a vicar. Or at least he used to be one before they defrocked him." She turns back to the Pastor. "Yes, I've done my research on you - especially after our last conversation. I know all about you."

The Pastor glares at the lady with the bag and retorts, "If you had done your research properly you would realise I was not defrocked but retired against my will." He turns to the customer and addresses him directly without lowering the tone of his voice - he wants the lady with the bag to hear everything he has to say.

"Well, I guess you must be the chairman of RLE Services PLC. I bet she doesn't realise who you are or I doubt she would be speaking to you. In her eyes successful business people like you, and corporate companies such as yours, are the spawn of Satan committed to the destruction of the planet. Has she been filling your time with her useless baggage of conspiracy flavoured crisps. Buy her a drink. It will keep her happy. Then we will go and have our conversation in the privacy of the lounge bar."

He turns away to place his regular order for a half of stout with the bar person, takes out a purse from inside his cassock and pays for it - he has no intention of allowing the chairman to buy him a drink.

He waits for the chairman to purchase the drink for the lady with the bag and then removes him as quickly as possible from the vicinity of the crazy woman, taking him from the bar into the quiet quarter of the lounge. There he chooses a couple of comfortable seats positioned at a side table in front of a window with views looking out onto the High Street.

They sit in silence, there is no-one else in the lounge - the Pastor scrutinises his new acquaintance. He seems a reasonable enough type. He smells truthful and there is no sour odour of deceit about him.

He finds this strange. The man was not portraying any of the characteristics he would have expected from the successful doyen of an internationally renowned PLC - rather he comes across more as the philosophical type, an artist maybe. The Pastor picks up his half pint of stout, takes a small sip, places the glass back on the table and decides to break the silence.

"You know I never used to drink - not for over forty years - I didn't have a clue what I was missing. The good Lord used to drink, now I know why. You are not what I was expecting. How do you see yourself. What do you identify as - obviously not as a successful business man - you don't look or smell like one."

The chairman smiles becoming thoughtful for a moment. This is the second time in one afternoon he has been asked to explain who or what he is. It used to be an easy question to answer, however, following the early morning meeting with the chief executive during which he found himself agreeing to take a sabbatical from his work, something changed within his perception of himself. Initially he had experienced of sense of loss, a feeling of grief as if losing a close friend. Part of himself had died when he divested himself, albeit temporarily, from his role of chairman. Now he realises he no longer feels comfortable identifying with being a successful businessman or the eminent chairman of a large internationally recognised business.

Yet there is no new identity replacing the old, he is stateless, he has no role. He feels slightly at a loss with the question being asked of him - 'who am I? - what am I now in this moment sitting in front of this man?'

A silence arises in him - a pause for reflection.

There is a mist around his eyes which forms into white petals flowing down to his feet - there is a sense of spring - a perception of a truth awaiting the discovery of summer. Without really considering what he is saying he speaks.

"I am on a sabbatical from my business seeking the truth?"

The Pastor looks momentarily stunned and laughs. "You seek the truth - the person responsible for the creation of a psychometric assessment tool based on the fabricated fiction of a drug addled alcoholic and who then proceeded to make a financial fortune from its use?"

There is an uncomfortable silence. It passes. The man takes out a letter from his pocket and hands it to the Pastor. "Please will you read this letter. It explains why I wanted to see you."

The Pastor takes the letter, places it on the table in front of him, puts a hand inside his cassock pocket removing a pair of horn-rimmed glasses, which he places carefully on his nose and over his ears. He picks up the letter and reads it carefully and slowly. Occasionally he makes an obfuscated grunt as he reads certain specific details. Finally he finishes, refolds the letter and places it on the table. He removes his glasses and peers at the man sitting opposite him.

"So when you find the truth what exactly are you going to do with it? Tell others? I have tried that - it doesn't work. I spent twenty-three years trying to help others discover a truth. The problem is no-one can be honest with themselves - they hide behind the lies they seek acceptance and affirmation for. Nobody lies well, you can smell it in their voice and through their bodies. You have to be in a possession of a good memory to lie well."

"But surely your congregation believed in the truth you provided them with?"

"They obviously did not or they would not have asked me to retire. Therein was their lie. Your Aunt believes you to be a truth-seeker on the path to becoming a truth-sayer. In the olden times a truth-sayer was called a prophet. Find me a prophet who has not had an unfortunate life.

"Very few people claim to seek the truth, and very few of their number really want to find the truth. Believe me for I am a truth-sayer and no-one wishes to hear my truth. I even once provided your company with the truth about your wretched psychometric assessment but all your company secretary did was threaten me with legal action."

The man looks confused for a moment. "I wasn't aware we had entered into any correspondence with you." He remains thoughtful before continuing. "However, at the time I was focussing on the strategic development of the business and had passed responsibility for the daily operational matters into the hands of my company secretary - I am sorry if we upset you in anyway..."

The Pastor chooses to ignore his comments and scrutinises the letter once more before returning his attention to the man opposite him.

"I was sorry to hear of the death of the Aunt, I was very fond of her - she was a deep and thoughtful person who had a beneficial influence upon everyone who came across her path. She lived her life with good sense tempered with humour. Nevertheless, with the exception of the occasional correspondence we did not remain in contact once I left the church."

He pauses and peers closely at the chairman. "Ah, I recognise you now, she used to bring you to the church as a boy - a rather taciturn creature with a propensity to draw the most peculiar pictures. You know some people would have described you as odd. Would such a description apply to you now I wonder.

"Today I was going to grind my axe against your truth. I was going to reveal to you the damage your company has inflicted on society by the misrepresentation of a symbol which has existed since the dawning of time. How one could imagine it was appropriate to make money out of imagery designed to freely help and guide people through the complexities of spiritual life is truly beyond me.

"Now I have met you I know you are at least, on one level, aware of the damage you have done. I also realise there is nothing more you can do with the truth of the lie. You appear to have passed beyond the life you were leading as a man of business, such a role no longer belongs to you - but maybe you are already aware of this? You also need to understand that whatever the truth is concerning your precious psychometric assessment, no-one will appreciate it or understand it - anything you discover will simply not be accepted by your ex-colleagues - you have lost your moral authority over them.

"I remember your parents as well - a rot was seeded into the fabric of the church when they joined us in the early years of their search for personal self-aggrandisement through, what did they call it - oh yes, inner self-contentment. They had the audacity to put themselves forward to be elders of the church without any comprehension of the esoteric nature of our way.

"Fortunately there were enough older members of the church at the time, your Aunt included, who voted in a different direction. They left the church in a huff and took a few younger members of the congregation with them - good riddance. That was the time when they appropriated the image of the cross above the altar of the church to use as the logo for their pathetic business peddling half-truths to people with more money than spiritual wisdom.

"We considered our options but felt there were no particular legal rights to a universal symbol that had existed since time immemorial, and anyway we didn't wish to draw any further attention to your parents, who regardless of their ill-conceived business remained quite popular amongst some of the congregation. Your Guardian proved me wrong when he registered his iteration of the image as a trademark. You compounded the error by adopting it as the framework for your psychometric assessment. Tell me do you ever worry about what other people think of you?"

The man opposite is thoughtful for a moment as he contemplates whether or not he has ever been concerned about what people think of him.

"I don't believe I have ever worried about what people thought of me. At school I was a loner - I never really got involved with the other students. They tried to bully me of course - I was different in their eyes and I certainly had no affinity to sport which was primarily all the Boarding School was interested in promoting. I had a little talent for art. They left me alone.

"It has been pretty much the same story throughout my life - I suppose I have always been a bit of an outsider - I like being the observer, I think this is why I was so successful in business, I could see what others couldn't observe."

"Then what was your intention behind the psychometric assessment tool you allowed to be developed under your personal direction?"

"I wanted to create something of value to society from the ashes of my parents' life. It was to be my legacy. At the time I believed the Symbolic Psychometric Personality Assessment had the potential to ease many of the world's humanitarian concerns regarding the full and satisfactory employment of its citizens." He pauses.

The Pastor considers him carefully before replying.

"Your answer reveals you do care about what others think of you. It seems quite clear to me that if you desire to leave a legacy you want people to consider you in a certain way and the fact you are concerned about finding the truth regarding your misguided attempts to create your legacy indicates this.

"Yet you claim to be an observer looking in from the outside and maybe you are. But what is an observer other than a person who is unable or not prepared to engage with anyone else in a meaningful way. Loners, observers, outsiders, however you wish to define yourself, are simply people hiding away from the truth of life - essentially they are selfish. It appears to me you have never really engaged with anyone other than yourself. Would you describe yourself as a selfish man?"

"I'm not sure I would and I am not sure I necessarily agree with your interpretation. I have engaged with many people throughout my life. I engaged with Aunt. I engage with my colleagues. I care about my employees..."

"Possibly you do - but where is the true engagement. Have you ever been close to someone, married even? Have you ever revealed your thoughts and emotions to anyone other than yourself?"

"No, I never had the time - I was focussing on my business."

"Then you have lost your way. To follow the line of truth requires your engagement with others on a much deeper and personal level than you appear to have done so far. It is not necessarily a comfortable journey but it is required nonetheless. Being an observer is not going to take you in any direction."

The Pastor pauses looking carefully to see if the man opposite is actually capable of digesting the truth. He sees him wince as if feeling something he has never tasted before.

"So, you sense the truth through your body. I sense the truth through smell. Very similar skills." He does not bother to explain what he has just said or wait for a response.

"The cross above our altar was the representation of a very old and ancient symbol which predated Christianity by many millennia. I find it ironic that this ancient image which meant so much to me and others as a guide in our personal search for truth has, regardless of my own failed attempts to disseminate the knowledge it revealed, ended up becoming an internationally recognised psychometric assessment tool, the creation of which was based, as I just previously said, on a series of non-sensical interpretations of its meaning conceived by a crazy drug addled alcoholic.

"In some respects I have to admire your dedicated handiwork even though it bears little relation to the actual truth. Especially the way in which you were able to justify your final interpretation through those pseudo-scientific research programmes undertaken by your psychologists.

"It is only recently that I managed finally to track down my successor and challenge her over her involvement in this matter.

"She had been outstaying her welcome with an old friend of hers in the city. I confronted her in the high street coffee bar. She didn't know who I was and was surprised when I introduced myself to her.

"I promised the meeting would be advantageous to her. I wasn't lying, I was endeavouring to give her an opportunity to be cleansed from some of the karmic debt she will have incurred during this lifetime. She was not particularly pleased to meet me.

"We had quite a philosophical debate. I will give you the crux of what was said, maybe it will help you realise the pointlessness of your quest and leave it to others who have more knowledge than you.

"I asked her why she had provided your company with a completely fabricated and fanciful interpretation of the symbol. She replied that what she had written was the truth as she perceived it and her words were divinely inspired by god. As far as she was concerned how your business development people decided to use her divine inspiration was not up to her - it was the will of the good lord.

"I pointed out the information she had concocted bore no relationship to the truth contained within the historical and esoteric information held within the archives of the church.

"She replied that as an older man there would probably be a degree of unconscious bias in how I perceived reality in relation to her. I told her I believed in the reality of truth and her truth was merely a falsehood.

"Her final comment before insisting I leave her alone was - 'likewise your truth may not be reality - where is the line between either truth or falsehood?'

"I have to say she was an extremely intelligent and captivating woman in her own way, and I began to understand why so many people had been 'taken in' by her. Including yourself."

"To be honest I only met her the once, at the wedding between her and the director of business development. Maybe I should go and talk to her as well."

The Pastor growled. "What for? Were you not listening to me. Your invention flew away from its loving parent a long time ago. You have no control over it now, it has developed a life of its own. I have a feeling you will never find her anyway - certainly not in this lifetime." He pauses and looks closely at the man.

"So, you say you are on a sabbatical - were you encouraged to become a Sabbatical? My guess is you won't be encouraged back if you are planning on throwing the proverbial baby out with the bath water. I haven't met your chief executive yet but I was planning to do so. Did you know he has just recently moved into our village. I was contemplating a warm welcome to my new neighbour - I am sure he will be surprised to meet me in the flesh."

The Pastor suddenly pauses, there is a revelation, a revealing of a truth that has been hiding behind what he now begins to realise is a deeply held obsession to expose the lie. It has consumed his life for far too many years. He has subconsciously identified with a sequence of events which have no significant meaning within his own journey. What had he been doing for all these years? Had he been asleep to himself?

By association he remembers a similar revelation twenty-three years ago whilst he was preparing to lead his final act of worship in the Church of Universal Values. Then it had taken the form of an existential question – 'what is the point of all and everything you have ever said and done?'

Now he has to conclude all his actions concerning the abhorrent interpretation of the Spiritualis Tabula Vitae Interiores have been pointless – his obsession has taken him away from his true destiny. There was no rightful indignation – he had merely been expressing the coarse emotional energy of an anger resulting from having been retired and had used this energy to provide his ordinary life with a meaning it no longer had.

His successor had most likely been accurate in her assessment of the situation, whatever had occurred was inspired by divine will. Regardless of anything he chose to do the truth would always remain available to those who sincerely searched for the way. It was no longer any of his business and to think so was purely an expression of arrogance.

It was inevitable - his role as a teacher and educator was drawing to a natural conclusion - it was for others to proceed along the path he himself had been traversing. Finally, it is time for him to complete the journey of life, on his own, toward the source of all being. He sighs...

"Probably meeting your chief executive and confronting him regarding this matter, as I have with you, is no longer relevant or appropriate. Having now met you it would seem that continuing to be concerned over your precious psychometric assessment is no longer worthy of my time or effort. There is nothing I can do to return the genie to the bottle as I am only slowly now beginning to realise – it is no longer my responsibility and probably it never was.

"I have been obsessing over this for far too long - as I said, your precocious child now has a life of its own and an individual path of destiny to follow. In the meantime I should return to the path and continue my own journey towards the source of all being without dragging my feet over this little fixation of mine.

"Nevertheless, I will probably go and visit your chief executive and welcome him to our village. I feel called to make peace with him – to atone for my past behaviour – though I doubt he will even remember or care about who I am – why should he? I appear to have developed an overweening sense of self-importance about who and what I am.

"I thank you for being the source of my enlightenment - in return let me give you some advice.

"You have a decision to make, continue with the lie and return to your habitual way of being or go on a journey to discover who and what you really are.

"I suggest you go to the Ashram and stay there for a while as your Aunt has recommended. You could well be surprised by what transpires. I once knew the Ashram's Guru quite well. He was the grandson of the Church of Universal Values' original founder who stayed at the Ashram whilst on a sabbatical mission to explore the foundation of Christian culture on the Indian subcontinent. He ended up staying there for ten years until he returned and founded the Church of Universal Values.

"The grandson decided to follow in his grandfather's footsteps and chose to remain there. He met your Aunt shortly after he arrived - they became very close friends. You will need to write to the Ashram to arrange approval for your visit. I will also write to the Guru telling him of your Aunt's death and your imminent arrival - a letter of introduction so he knows who you are, and the baggage you bring with you.

"Now if you don't mind I need some space and would like to finish my drink in peace and quiet, on my own."

The Pastor turns his gaze away from the Sabbatical, cups both his hands around the half pint glass which now retains two thirds of the treasured stout, and gazes down into the dark brown liquid meditatively.

The Sabbatical is surprised by the Pastor's abrupt ending to their meeting - it is not something he has experienced before as he is the person generally in the chair determining when a meeting should be concluded. Not only does he appear to have lost his persona, he no longer has any sense of being in control over his life.

He is about to say something but can find no words to convey his thoughts. Instead he feels compelled to stand up. As he does so he leaves his drink unfinished on the table experiencing a peculiar obligation not to disturb the Pastor in his rumination. He tries to say goodbye but all he manages is a murmured thank you as he makes his way through the lounge and out of the front door into the High Street, inordinately confused by all that has transpired.

The Pastor hears him leave, turns to look out of the window and sighs again. This particular outcome was not the one he had been expecting from this afternoon's meeting. There is a letter to write, one he has been putting off ever since he had learnt of the old woman's death.

He sits quietly for a further fifteen minutes contemplating the remainder of his stout. Once he has finished his drink he stands up, returns the glass to the bar, glares at the women with the bag (who appears to be fast asleep slumped over a table), walks back through the lounge and out of the door into the courtyard where he unchains his bicycle and rides home.

As is customary on his return to the bungalow he goes straight out into the garden - the vegetable patch is in need of a little clearing and the flower beds are in want of a tidying up. He strolls across to the tool shed and selects some sturdy garden gloves, a hoe, a fork, a spade, a pair of shears, and together with a wicker basket, places them in a wheelbarrow.

He manoeuvres the wheelbarrow carefully down to the vegetable plot at the bottom of the garden where he endeavours to undertake his chores mindfully, being conscious of the fact he is continuously losing himself within the association of his thoughts concerning the letter he needs to write.

Eventually in the later afternoon he decides stop what he is doing and harvest some vegetables for his supper. Today he feels the need for a green meal so selects some broad beans, chard and spinach. These he places in the wicker basket to take back to the kitchen after returning the tools and gloves to the garden shed.

He slowly walks back to the bungalow and into his kitchen. There he cleans the vegetables and prepares them for cooking. He sautés them in a little butter and water and serves them onto his plate with a little side dish of radish and spring onion. He thanks God for his food and, as always, endeavours consume his food and not his thoughts. Today it takes much longer than usual to conclude his meal.

After he finishes eating he sits contemplatively for a moment before clearing up his plates and placing them in the kitchen sink. He washes them carefully before drying and returning them to their allocated spaces on the Welsh dresser.

He walks slowly into his living room where he sits down at his writing bureau, opens the lid and removes several sheets of white bonded paper. He picks up a dark red fountain pen with gold plated nib and fills the cartridge with green ink. He pauses for a moment and prays out aloud a slightly amended version of his early morning mantra, *'dear lord let the inspiration of your divine love be revealed within these words.'* He begins to write.

My dear old friend

It has been several years since we last corresponded and I am writing to you today regarding several matters we have discussed previously in the past and upon which you indicated a wish to be kept informed of in the future.

Firstly, our concern over the use of the Spiritualis Tabula Vitae Interiores was justified. However I now fully comprehend there is nothing you nor I can do to ameliorate the evil of its manipulated dissemination.

As is inevitable with any path of truth revealed to humanity, the way has been hidden temporarily out of sight. Nevertheless, as we both know, the Truth will arise once more in a resurrected form when it is the time for it to be rediscovered. In the meantime it is our duty to keep the embers of its essence within our hearts in the hope that we, or our successors, will find a way to rekindle its everlasting fire.

You also asked me to keep you apprised of the ongoing wellbeing of our sister in truth, your beloved. Whilst I have not been in direct communication with her for some years it has come to my attention she finally departed from this mortal plane several weeks ago.

She was very old, yet obviously retained her spiritual acuity and joie de vivre to the very end. Let us rejoice at her return to the universal source of all being rather than be consumed with any sadness. As we both understand the emotion of grief merely represents our own personal regret of having been left behind temporarily.

I was informed of her death by none other than the Chairman of RLE Incorporate PLC, the primary instigator behind the psychometric excrement derived from the corruption of the Spiritualis Tabula Vitae Interiores.

He is the sole executor of her estate and she requested that he should inform me of her death. At first I was confused as to why she would have appointed him as her executor. It was only when I met him I recognised him as the young boy she had looked after for many years after his parents, the founders of the Religion of Least Effort, had died. As you know she always thought of him as the child she never had.

As a young boy he had a very peculiar talent for drawing pictures of events he was not aware of having actually occurred and of circumstances that had not yet happened. In a letter she left for him (and which I have read) she requested he should bring her ashes to your Ashram to be scattered in the Hindu water ceremony for death. She also suggested he should stay at the Ashram for a little while - she particularly wanted him to learn the truth regarding his appropriation of the Spiritualis Tabula Vitae Interiores and rectify any damage caused as a result.

I have examined the boy and found him to be suffering from remorse. In the letter our sister indicates a belief that he is a seeker of truth - I would affirm her belief. She also believes he may be a truth-sayer. This I cannot confirm though you will be able to determine this for yourself.

I have advised him not only to bring the ashes to you but to also follow the advice of our sister and reside with you the Ashram for a while after the ceremony has been undertaken. If he comes to you he will have determined to seek out the truth.

Whilst I am conscious that whatever you actualise within him will be tempered with compassion, do not be too gentle with him, he needs the shock. He may be the one you have been waiting for.

I remain as always,

A true friend.

The Pastor sighs and puts down his pen to consider the written letter. Finding it to be good he places it in an envelope. He goes to the top drawer of the bureau and pulls out an old leather address book. He opens it and finding the relevant entry picks up his pen once more to write the address for the Ashram on the envelope, thus completing the task which has consumed his attention since leaving the hotel.

He closes up the desk and places the addressed envelope on top of the bureau. Tomorrow he will ride his bike into the village to the post office and make the payment to send his letter by special delivery.

He stands up and walks into his little chapel for his evening meditation which he concludes by reciting his personal adaptation of the liturgy for Compline taken from the book of common prayer culminating with his final prayer for the day:

Guide in my waking, O Lord, and guard me in my sleeping; that awake I may watch with Christ, and asleep I may rest in peace.

The almighty and merciful Lord, Father, Son, and Holy Spirit, bless me and keep me and all fellow men. Amen.

He returns to the kitchen, composes a list of the chores which need to be undertaken the following morning and pins it to his notice board next to the fridge. He prepares his muesli with the yoghurt and stewed fruit, places it into the fridge and retires to his bed.

Chapter 6 - The Politician

'Through the corruption of thought
a new reality is created.'

The alarm in the bedroom of his penthouse suite overlooking the river dividing the somewhat overpopulated city is set for 5.26am. His reason for doing so is really quite simple - it amuses him. It also means he can inform any interviewer, should they be impertinent enough to inquire, that he always gets up to commence his daily routine prior to 5.30am. It is important, at least in his own mind, to present the image of a person dedicated to his craft, a chap who doesn't mind hard work, the friendly guy who lives next door who is a man of the people, someone who understands the true nature of what it means to have to graft for a living. This is the image he has honed to perfection throughout his ongoing and undoubtably successful career as a politician, a profession he chose over his equally successful vocation as the leading partner of the city's largest international consultancy firm.

He is wealthy due to a series of clever investments he made when he was younger. What he managed to do was not illegal in anyway shape or form - certainly nothing which at a later date could be described by his political enemies as insider trading. His strategy was relatively simple; there were fellow students from his university days who he identified as future potential scions of industry. He invested his money privately in the business' they involved themselves with - and then left them alone. He never approaches them for any contributions towards his political activities - 'attention to the finer details' is the daily mantra he lives by. Neither does he grant them any political license and there are no favours or graces awarded for his investments with them. Lobbying he leaves to his politically naive colleagues; his competitors who will invariably fall at the final hurdle because of their all-consuming avarice.

He himself is not greedy, merely ambitious; a compulsive winner who has never lost whether it was rugby or rowing at The Boarding School and

University, business dealings as a consultant in the city, or mastering the navigation of those early political strategies for which he has now been rewarded with a seat at the cabinet table.

Politics is just another sport - and he was born to be this generation's overall winning competitor. He is shortly going to fulfil his destiny and take first prize in the ultimate political game, though no-one yet realises he has entered the tournament - it is a secret he keeps to himself for he himself is the only person, other than his mother, who can be trusted with such sensitive information.

He is mostly disinterested in the internecine conspiracy theories whispered amongst the party unfaithful in the tea rooms and bars of parliament. Neither is he overly worried about the current interminable conjecture concerning the Prime Minister's increasing senility apropos his ability to lead the party into the next general election. The fact his senile old 'friend' has been incapable of tying his proverbial shoelaces for the previous year has been concealed from the prying eyes of the trolls by the machinations of the old man's secret cabal of personal advisors, of which, quite naturally, he is the chief. Even the deputy prime minister had been kept unaware of how serious the situation was until very recently.

The deputy prime minister is his only potential rival in the oncoming tourney. Propitiously the honourable member has been foolish enough to break cover, stirring up unnecessary concerns amongst the party's unemployable backbenchers thereby heightening their ever-increasing angst.

Fortunately, the imbecilic odious toad will not stand a chance of winning the greatest prize in politics - for there are a few dodgy investments even the whips are unaware of which will defenestrate him once they are divulged to the press.

Not that he will personally disclose them himself - he is not of the leaking type, for it is always fairly obvious where the poisonous tittle tattle of another person's financial indiscretions have originated from - 'attention to the finer details'; the revelations he himself have inspired will be geared quite unintentionally by people who have no obvious connection to him - there will be no fingers pointing in his direction.

Anyway, if the rumours are true, the deputy prime minister has managed to disrupt enough of his disgruntled fellow party members to submit the sufficient number of letters to the executive party council expressing a lack of conviction in their prime minister's leadership of the party to enforce a motion of no confidence. He himself will of course support the senile geriatric to the end of his tenure, as no doubt the deputy prime minister will also; nevertheless, the Prime Minister will inevitably be ousted within six months by the braying cabal of delinquent honourables. Obviously, the traitorous knife in the Prime Minister's back will not bear the hallmarks of his assassin's DNA...

As far as he is concerned there are only two types of honourable member: the sycophantic, pathetically wet liberal elitists who enter the house with the ingenuous belief they will achieve something of benefit for the plebeian caucus of voters who cast their vote for them; and the narcissistic power-hungry psychopaths who desire complete adoration from, and the total control over, the aforesaid plebeian caucus of voters.

In his less than humble opinion, he falls into neither camp - he is their natural born leader, immensely intelligent, well-educated and more than capable of running the country successfully on a sound economic basis for the benefit of everyone who can be bothered to recognise their true and rightful place in society. He does not believe in the liberal fantasy of meritocracy - as far as he is concerned people are born with set preferences, abilities and functions and should be content with the circumstance they have been allotted in life.

On this particular morning when his alarm rings out confirming the arrival of a new dawn. he has already been awake for a little while pondering the desideratum for the following twelve hours. He immediately rolls onto his back, sits upright, throws the duvet towards the foot of the bed, places his left hand next to his pelvis and swings around his legs to place his feet on the light oak parquet flooring.

He takes a moment to allow the pressure of the smooth oaken wood to register sensuously upon his skin. He stands up and walks over towards the window where the full-length antique boudoir French mirror he purloined off his father after he had moved him into the All Care Private Country Nursing Home and Rehabilitation Centre is positioned. He takes a moment to scrutinise his reflection.

He is pleased with what he sees; strong accentuated calf muscles, firm thighs, well sculptured buttocks, a more than adequately sized and well-formed penis, a slim waist, a well delineated six pack, muscular chest, and the arms of a fit and healthy oarsman. His face is strong, angular with the rugged handsome look of a person comfortable in their own skin, with a strong mouth, aquiline nose, crystal clear blue eyes, all topped off with a full head of thick curly dark-brown close-cropped hair.

"God, I am so fucking handsome." he voices out aloud. God, as is his wont, continues to ignore the spurious aspirations of the Politician. For it was god, after all, who enabled his good lucks, along with the creation of a suitably sanguine society most likely to appreciate them.

He strides over to his ensuite bathroom, urinates, masturbates, and takes a four-minute cold shower.

After brushing his teeth he returns to his boudoir and opens the built in closet to select the clothes he intends to wear for today's assignments. He singles out a fresh pair of merino dark grey socks and boxer shorts, bespoke monogrammed white shirt, and a hand tailored single breast suit in a grey/blue cotton/cashmere blend. Both the shirts and suits are made especially for him by his personal Savile Row tailor.

Having dressed he walks out of his bedroom down the hall to the large open planned kitchen and living area where his little security minder will have prepared him a freshly ground coffee with oat milk, his ice-cold ginger shot infused with turmeric, and mashed avocado with kalamata olives on two slices of artisan sourdough toast. His personal dietician considers this to be the healthiest possible breakfast for his body type. As he breaks his fast he will glance through the daily newspapers his little security minder will have already fetched for him.

If you were worrying about our politician's ability to empathise with the rabble of poverty-stricken voters in his city constituency, rest assured, he is fully aware of the price of a mass factory produced loaf of bread baked using the Chorleywood baking process and a tin of budget baked beans. No, he has never fallen into that particular odious trap where an interviewer talking about the cost-of-living crisis is impertinent enough to inquire whether or not he knows the price of individual essential basic staples such as frozen tomato pizzas. He is also fully aware of current housing costs and the generally pitiable average incomes his constituents are required to survive upon.

Today is going to be a busy day even though there is nothing scheduled in his official office diary other than that he is spending some quality time with his family. Today is the day where he gets to dot the proverbial I's and cross the proverbial T's, so to speak, and ensure there are no ghastly little gremlins (or relatives) waiting to trip him up as he travels ever onwards along the road towards victory.

Firstly, though, there is the small matter of ensuring the Chief Executive of RLE Services PLC recognises the importance of appropriately vanishing the errant Chairman of the company permanently from the board of directors - so a little ad-hoc meeting is in order. Fortunately the RLE head office is just across the river from where his penthouse is situated and the Chief Executive likes to start his day early at 6.30am, so he will arrange to drop by and greet him at the door. A little phone call is all that will be necessary to ensure he is aware of the impending visit.

He finishes his breakfast and moves over to the living area out of earshot from his little security minder, picks up his personal cell phone, finds the appropriate contact details and taps the call button.

"Good morning, it's your esteemed next-door neighbour, your local member of parliament and secretary of state here. I thought I would drop by in a few minutes, 6.30 to be precise, and have a friendly catch up with my valued constituent - off the record of course - a little check in to see how your business is holding up within the current economic climate. Nothing for you to worry about - your government contracts are perfectly safe - well they are for the moment anyway. I will meet you at the front and we can have a little stroll together by the river. I will have my little security minder with me." He finishes the call without bothering to wait for a response. He knows the Chief Executive will be waiting at the door - he can't afford not to.

He walks back over to the kitchen area and notices the little security minder is pouring himself another cup of coffee.

"No time for coffee - we've got places to go and people to see. All personal stuff - no government business today. Now what have I told you about the need to be on top of your game and available at the drop of a needle. Early birds and all that. I expect efficiency at all times, otherwise you are of no use to me - you know what I mean - we can always find a replacement for the morning shift." He registers the look of shock on the little security minder's face and bursts into laughter.

"For god's sake man, don't look so startled, I'm only teasing you - you're doing a relatively reasonable job so far - I don't want to replace you just yet. Now be a good person and get my car, we are off to see some relatives of mine later, but first we are going to drop in and say hi to the chief executive of RLE Services PLC. He will be waiting for us at the front of their head office at 6.30. You can drive."

They arrive at the head office car park at 6.28am and as expected the Chief Executive is already waiting for them. This pleases the Politician for he likes punctuality - if he says meeting at 6.30am he expects people to be awaiting his arrival at least several minutes before then - early birds and all that.

Instead of waiting for the little security minder to follow the standard protocol of opening the door for him, the Politician opens it himself and steps out. He pauses for a moment by the side of the door before leaning back in to provide instructions to the little security minder.

"I am going for a short walk by the river with this little friend of mine. Go and park the car and then you can do your little bit of minding by following us at a discrete distance. We are extremely unlikely to get into any trouble this early in the morning."

He walks over to where the Chief Executive is waiting for him. He extends his right arm out proffering the formality of a handshake. It's not something he generally encourages but it seems appropriate this morning. Any way he quite likes the man although he is significantly less malleable than the odious overweight toad who preceded him in the role. Having said that, since his recent divorce the Chief Executive has become obsessively focussed on increasing the overall share value of his business. This has definitely played favourably into the Politician's hand in their more recent dealings with each other.

The Chief Executive reciprocates appropriately and points over to the far end of the car park where there is a gate leading out to the river path. They walk towards it with the little security minder following fifteen paces behind.

It is the Politician who starts the conversation.

"How are you finding single life? Personally I have never understood why people feel the need to get married, especially when over 40% will get divorced and the majority of the remainder spend their servitude to each other in misery. Didn't you find it immensely inconvenient? Obviously she did - isn't she now the senior partner of her law firm. I would never trust anyone in the legal profession. Anyway at least you now have more time to focus on the success of your business."

The Chief Executive allows himself a wry smile. He has known the Politician for long enough now to appreciate his need to play the game of one-upmanship to prove himself as the dominant force in any particular conversational transaction - he will go along with it for the moment.

"You forget, I am a lawyer by trade." He replies mildly.

"Exactly. We understand each other fully. Your predecessor as Chief Executive was a particularly unctuous man yet he had a trait I found extremely useful - he was a people pleaser who thrived on the validation of others. He always found a way to ensure that any concerns raised by those who truly mattered were resolved in such a way they left feeling a warm sense of security - that everything was completely under control.

"Now, if you don't mind me saying so, you are a completely different kettle of fish, extremely competent no doubt but certainly not a people pleaser. Nevertheless, I should congratulate you on managing to get your Chairman to take a sabbatical. I assume I was right in thinking he was displaying an unhealthy interest in the unfortunate incident which occurred at the Four Feathers Public House?"

"Indeed he was and still is. The incident appears to have placed a bee in his bonnet regarding the efficacy of the SPPA and the way it is being applied in the workplace. He believes it is being used inappropriately to the detriment of all those undertaking the assessment. Naturally his behaviour in this matter is of concern to us all, and as you know I tried to keep him unaware of the murder case for as long as possible - the SPPA is one of my company's most successful products, underpinning many of the services we provide - including our contracts with your government.

"Unfortunately, he appears to have taken it upon himself to use his sabbatical to seek out some sort of truth to prove his point - he feels the SPPA is solely his responsibility, his legacy to the world. I am keeping an eye on the situation to ensure he doesn't do anything which frightens our shareholders."

"Good god man, why on earth would he want to meddle with the truth? Does he really believe anyone will be interested in what he has to say? In my experience nobody really wants to know the truth, especially if there is a price to pay for it - and his meddling in this matter could cost you a great deal. Trust me I am a politician and I know about such things. Politics is a business based on telling people what they want to hear, an illusional vision of the future which will never actually be realised. People believe in the possibility of a better tomorrow and truth doesn't have anything to do with it. Ultimately your SPPA is a political tool leading people to believe they can have a better future, a future in which they will feel contented."

The Politician pauses for a moment and stands still looking at the Chief Executive in askance. The Chef Executive is fully aware of the look but is unsure what question is being asked of him. After a few moments he decides on a reply.

"I agree with your sentiments, nevertheless our Chairman is a highly principled man and always has been. In some respects it was those principles which made the business what it is today and led to the development of the SPPA. At the moment, even if he is on sabbatical, he is still technically our Chairman."

The politician responds immediately.

"I am not sure why you insist on supporting this man's behaviour. Being highly principled and running a publicly listed company like yours no longer correlates. It was useful perhaps to have a highly principled person at the helm when the company was not listed. However, following the merger with ROC Services this ceased to be the case.

"You yourself now have a responsibility to your investors for what is perceived to be a flourishing and prosperous business - waving the flag for our country - an exemplar to our overseas friends as to how an international corporation should be run.

"You currently have the support of the Government. This is reflected in the number of contracts you have won from us. Let us hope it stays that way. I would not like this little storm in a teacup to brew into anything beyond the saucer it is placed upon. If the share price of your business were to fall significantly because of the negative behaviour of your Chairman, I cannot see how the Government could justify continuing its ongoing contracts with you - if you follow my meaning.

"As you are aware, before I entered politics I was an extremely successful business consultant in the City. Let me give you a piece of commercial advice - off the record obviously. Attention to the finer details is the order of the day. You as a lawyer should be more than fully aware of this.

"Anyway, your Chairman is a finer detail and you really should not risk the future direction of your business with him on the bridge - so to speak. Unnecessary risks are a pointless form of gambling. It is time to replace your Chairman. I know the board will support such a move if you propose it. I don't believe it will be too difficult to get the shareholders on-side.

"Now I really must be going - things to do, people to see. I look forward to hearing who the new Chair will be."

With the final Damoclesian statement lingering in the air the Politician turns away from the Chief Executive and walks briskly back down the river path toward the car park with the little security minder scuttling behind him.

When they reach the car park he turns to the little security minder and orders him to hand over the car key fob. On receiving it, he unlocks the door and jumps into the driving seat. He beckons the little security minder to get into the front passenger seat next to him. Once this manoeuvre has been effectuated to his satisfaction he presses the push-button ignition, places the car into gear, puts his foot down and speeds back over the bridge across the river to his Penthouse. On reaching the secure underground parking entrance he brings the car to halt and passes the key fob over to the little security minder.

"Park the car and come back upstairs. We have a few hours grace before we need to set about on our travels again - you could brew up some more coffee to make up for the one I forced you to miss earlier and wait for me in the lobby by the front door. Take one of the newspapers if you want. I need some peace and quiet and I don't wish to be disturbed. There are some items from my ministerial red box I need to look through again. I also need to prepare for tomorrow's morning round of media interviews. You just relax, you'll be busy enough later. You see I am not really that bad to work for am I - I'm actually really quite generous."

Unlike many of his colleagues he relishes the cut and thrust of the morning media interview rounds. In fact he is considered the safest pair of hands capable of catching the most devious of balls thrown by an interviewer - as always preparation and attention to the finer details is the order of the day. To play the rounds effectively you have to be aware of all those little aside issues likely to crop up over and beyond his ministerial brief (which of course he is fully on top of). Naturally, he has a posse of special political advisers and interns to advise him and he will utilise their savoir faire to ensure he has truly covered all of the finer details. However, he generally finds their counsel neither sharp nor quick enough to keep pace with his own dazzling intellect.

It is 11.30am when he finally calls his little security minder from the lobby and instructs him to run and fetch the car.

"I will meet you downstairs by the front door. We are off on a little jaunt to the All Care Private Country Nursing Home and Rehabilitation Centre to have a little chat with my progenitor and to ensure the director of the clinic is ready to greet his new guest who we will be delivering later - he is expecting us to be there by 12.30pm. You will drive - I will sit in the back, I have a little script for tomorrow's interviews which requires some minor adjustments."

The All Care Private Country Nursing Home and Rehabilitation Centre was established in an old country manor house within four acres of garden fifteen years ago. It is situated just two miles south of the little market town some thirty miles north of the somewhat overpopulated city which the Politician is the parliamentary representative for.

It was founded by one of his old university alumni who has since gone on to open four more such exclusive and expensive establishments designed only to be frequented by an extravagantly wealthy clientele or their relatives. One of the key benefits for its patrons are its security and confidentiality protocols.

Behind the large picturesque stone boundary walls there is an elaborate surveillance system ensuring inmates cannot get out (without permission and in the company of personal attendants), and no-one else can get in (especially the prying press eager to discover the identity of its inmates). It is, of course, regulated and meets the highest standards expected by the CQC. The staff are thoroughly vetted, well recompensed for their employment, and display intense loyalty to the organisation they work for.

His mother had divorced his father many years ago after discovering the hyper-sexed vitiator expressing the full extent of his libido on top of her best friend in the marital bed. This was during a party to celebrate their tenth wedding anniversary. Following the divorce she had gone on to marry a wealthy but childless landowner who was prepared to take on and acknowledge both the Politician and his sister as if they were his own. However, the stepfather found this easier to achieve with the pair of them out of sight and mind, so he happily sanctioned their attendance at The Boarding School.

His mother had taken to her new role as wife of a respectable and wealthy landowner by developing and taking on the appropriate airs and graces expected from such an elevated station. She forbade her children to have anything more to do with their original progenitor or her younger sister (who she considered to be of extremely poor repute) - they had the opportunity of a new life providing them with unlimited opportunity, and thereby shared with her the responsibilities of ensuring they met the standards expected by the select members of their newly acquired social elite.

His stepfather died shortly after he took on his first consultancy role in the city. His mother inherited the whole estate.

When he decided to enter politics his she advised him to re-establish some form of relationship with his actual male progenitor - the press would be bound to find him and rake up the dirt if the Politician was successful in Government. So, he re-established contact with his father and made himself invaluable to his life.

The old man was beginning to suffer from dementia. It was only a matter of time before the Politician had persuaded the senile old fool to give him enduring power of attorney. Six years ago he used this power effectively to sell his progenitor's property as the dementia became increasingly pronounced and, calling in an old favour from his alumni, the old incompetent was secured a place as a permanent resident of the All Care Private Country Nursing Home and Rehabilitation Centre.

His father will soon be joined by his aunt, who's destiny is also to become a long-term resident at the home. His mother was convinced her lunatic of a sister would shortly become one of those finer details needing to be dealt with - she had just been made homeless for the fourth time. Out of sound and out of the media's mind. He would be responsible for dictating their narrative to the world - the one about the benevolent son and nephew who had managed and arranged for their long-term care in a place where their needs would be carefully monitored and catered for.

Obviously, he is more than aware he is paying for a level of care the majority of his constituents can only dream of for themselves or their loved ones. The lack of affordable social care of any discernible quality for the lower echelons of society is a major political issue and the simple fact he had the wealth to bypass the pathetic provisions of the state could potentially be seen as being out of touch with the proletariat.

His argument to any potential protagonist was simple - he had the resources, both the progenitor's and his own, to pay for the care, and why would he therefore place an additional burden, however small, on a national system paid for by taxpayers, a system increasingly in danger of collapse under the strain of current demand. Those who could pay should pay to relieve the unnecessary burden put upon the state - he was providing an exemplary example.

They arrive at the gates of the All Care Private Country Nursing Home and Rehabilitation Centre at 12.15pm and after the little security minder had gained admission the Politician was pleased to find the director of the clinic waiting for him in the car park.

The little security minder drove over to the front entrance of the building and stopped the car. The Politician waited in the back. The little security minder turned around, he was expecting the Politician to get out of the car, like he had in the morning. The Politician growls at him.

"You know what is expected of you. Get out and open my door for god's sake. Surely you realised this was a meeting requiring the standard protocols. I am sat in the rear seat for god's sake - you must always open the door for me when I am in the back. Now do as you're told and make sure you stand respectfully as I get out. Then you can go and park the car and wait for my return. I will be an hour or so. When you see me come out bring the car around, get out and open the rear door for me to get in.

"These are really the simple duties you need to get used to if you are going to be useful to me. You need to be on top of your job like I am on top of mine. Do that and we will get on fine." He feigns a small smile of encouragement towards the little security minder as he hurries out of the driver seat and opens the nearside rear passenger door which is currently adjacent to the awaiting director of the clinic.

The Politicians alights the car gracefully and walks purposefully toward the director of the clinic who has proffered his hand toward the Politician in anticipation of a handshake. The Politician notices the hand and decides to ignore it - the man needs to understand his position in relation to his own. Instead he smiles by way of greeting.

The director of the clinic looks confused for a moment and lowers the proffered hand in resignation, appropriately realising his status in relation to the man he is greeting. Instead he indicates toward the door and allows the Politician to proceed before him through the entry and into the building's reception area. Once inside the lobby the Politician turns toward the director of the clinic.

"We need to have a conversation in private before I see my father. I need an update on his condition and long-term prognosis. There are also some other private discussions we need to have regarding the forthcoming arrival of my aunt to your establishment."

"Of course, of course. We are here to oblige. If you would like to follow me to my office, we will be private there. You know we take our patient confidentiality seriously here."

The Politician is unimpressed with the answer. "You know, in my line of work when someone says something like that we tend to believe the opposite."

The director of the clinic leads him through reception to a door with a large sign notifying anyone who approached it - 'Staff only beyond this point'. The director of the clinic punches in a code on the secure lock and opens the door, holds it open allowing the Politician to step through before him.

They walk down a corridor which would not look out of place in a relatively upmarket and affluent hotel. There is a thick beige woollen carpet, the walls are painted a in a high-quality light magnolia paint punctuated with the type of original works of art produced by second rate interior designers.

They arrive in front of a door at the end of the corridor on which there is a light oak sign bearing the inscription - 'Director and Clinical Manager' - it also has a security lock with a card reader. He waits for the director to wave his security pass over the reader and once again allows the door to be opened for him. With the appropriate courtesies achieved he proceeds through the door.

The office is a large Georgian room with non-original light oak panelling. It has a bay window looking out over the well-manicured gardens. The director's large Victorian desk is situated adjacent to the left-hand wall in a position where the occupant can look out of the window. On the right-hand wall is a large set of wooden shelves housing an assortment of different medical journals dating back over many years. There is a Chesterfield Mallory Flat Wing Queen Anne High Back Wing Chair behind the desk and two in front of it.

"I'm surprised you get anything done in here if this is the level of comfort you bestow upon yourself." The Politician comments.

The director smiles bashfully. "Actually, this room is only used to meet our most important clients, people like yourself, and potential customers. I normally work with my team in the general office down the corridor. Thank you for coming in to see us today - we are always delighted when our most important patrons drop by. Now I appreciate you are a very busy person so tell me how can we help you today?"

The Politician is beginning to be annoyed by the continuing sycophantic inauthentic oily customer service dialogue the director is spewing in his direction. Time to put him in his place - the silly little man is trying to rise above his station in life. He decides to put on his neutral non-emotional political face - the one he generally reserves for the more serious of his media interviews - it unsettles the questioner.

"I will ignore that question, you know full well why I am here - to see my father and to finalise arrangements for handing over my aunt into your care. Efficiency is the order of the day here. I have a limited amount of time and I am obviously concerned about my father's welfare and his ongoing care. I would like an update and prognosis of his condition. It has been a while since I last saw him."

The Politician is pleased to see the director is beginning to look uncomfortable. And indeed the director is. Whilst he is used to dealing with the upper echelons of society the politician is different from the majority of the home's other clientele. They generally regard him with the degree of awe quite naturally reserved for such a highly skilled clinician such as himself who has been entrusted with the ongoing custody of their relatives. He prides himself on being able to gauge the needs and requirements of all his customers - nevertheless, he always struggles to understand the Politician's needs - what is his real motivation for visiting today?

The Politician observes the director looking at him quizzically - he can guess what the silly little man is thinking.

"My motivation is simple. I have a responsibility for my father's welfare which I take very seriously. I obviously want to ensure he is getting the best possible care as he lives out his final years. I don't come here very often -

you advised me that my visits should be infrequent and so I have dutifully followed your advice. So let me ask you again - how is my father?"

The director cannot remember having ever dispensed such guidance to the Politician but chooses not to respond contrarily to the point being made. Instead he assumes the calm personae of the professional clinician with the hope it will ameliorate the atmosphere of what is already becoming an awkward meeting. He wishes to be regarded as a proficient clinician and manager, worthy of at least some respect from this man who at the moment appears to be regarding him with low esteem. He speaks slowly and precisely.

"As you are aware when your father first came to us we diagnosed him as having Lewy body dementia. We are continuing to treat this with Acetylcholinesterase inhibitors. The treatment is reducing the impact of the dementia, and the other physical conditions associated with this condition. His speech is slow, however, his intellect appears relatively undiminished though he frequently becomes confused.

"Unfortunately, as is often the case with this form of dementia, we believe he is beginning to present schizophrenic tendencies. The psychotic dimensions are relatively clear. He displays persecutory delusions, religious delusions, grandiose delusions, for example he believes he is one of the country's leading politicians who has been incarcerated here because he knows too much about how the country is really being run," - he pauses for a the briefest of seconds to appreciate the look of shock on the Politicians face before continuing -

"and erotomaniac delusions - which will probably come as no surprise to you. His behaviour can be erratic; we have allocated him a personal carer and put systems in place to monitor him at all times. In terms of his long term prognosis it is unlikely he could return home without an extensive care package put in place for him - we can of course arrange this for you if you so wish. Whilst he is an old man suffering a fair amount of infirmity, he may yet survive a few more years."

The director glances at the Politician hoping he has generated the desired response. He appears to have done so successfully as the Politician glances back at the director with a facial expression which now conveys the undoubtable concern of a dutiful relative who has just received unfortunate news regarding a loved one from a highly skilled medical practitioner.

"Well this is indeed sad to hear. Obviously he will need to remain here for the foreseeable future. My mother, his ex-wife will not be willing look after him - personal history and all that, and unfortunately I am not in a position to do so either. Neither are there any other relatives who would be prepared to take on the responsibility for his long-term care. We have the financial resources to pay for his ongoing treatment here and I can only thank you for the care and attention you have given him to date. How is he today? I would like to see him whilst I am here. It will be a long time before I can come again - matters of state, so to speak."

"Unfortunately we have had to return him to his room under supervision. He was in the communal lounge this morning and there was an inappropriate incident involving one of our elderly long term female residents. He believed she fancied him. He placed his hands over her breasts and started to kiss her. I understand he placed his tongue inside her mouth. She bit it - not hard enough to cause any damage, but it was evidently quite painful. Yes of course you may see him but I am not sure you will get much sense out of him today. I will take you to his room once we have finished here." He waits for a response from the Politician who is now looking at him thoughtfully.

"There is the other matter - my mother's sister. I am due to collect her from the old coach house hotel in town later this afternoon and bring her in to you for assessment. I am concerned she will arrive here somewhat disorientated. She has recently been made homeless again, the fourth time, and we are not sure what the state of her mental health is. Sadly, she was estranged from our family for many years regardless of our attempts to bring her into our lives. Thankfully, at long last, she has finally reached out to us for assistance – a cry for help so to speak.

"We obviously want to do what's best for her even if it means she remains a long-term resident with you. My mother is quite elderly now - her sister is much younger by a fair number of years. My mother no longer has the energy to take on such a responsibility and I am not convinced my aunt has the wherewithal to look after herself - obviously your assessment team will confirm one way or another.

"I am willing to pay for her residential care here for as long as necessary - I trust you understand our needs?"

The Politician looks at the director pointedly awaiting a suitable response. He finds the return of a sycophantic expression on the director's face a pleasure to behold, and the appropriate acknowledgement is not long coming.

"Rest assured, our assessment will be thorough and if we believe there is the slightest risk of harm we will advise you accordingly. Meanwhile she can stay with us for as long as necessary. We will ensure she is cared for suitably. Is there anything else I can help you with today."

The Politician smiles - there is no warmth intended.

"Yes, there is one last thing. As a Politician and leading member of the Government I receive a great deal of attention from the media. It has been brought to my attention they have discovered, regardless of the veracity of your confidentiality protocols, that my father is a patient here. I don't know how they found out - do you perchance?"

He pauses for a moment; it is a rhetorical question and he does not intend to provide an opportunity for the director to reply. He waits until he sees the director about to open his mouth before continuing.

"No, no, you don't need to try and justify yourself - whatever has happened has happened and the damage can't be undone - the horse has bolted beyond the stable door. I have been forewarned from a variety of reliable sources stories concerning my father's health and wellbeing will reported in the tabloid newspapers tomorrow. Now, whilst I expect to receive a certain degree of personal scrutiny from the media, my family should not be harassed as a result of my political status - or the failure of your confidentiality protocols.

"There is no doubt I will be asked a number of impenitent questions concerning my father's health and care package in tomorrow's morning media interviews. Obviously I would prefer to be answering questions regarding my own ministerial brief. I will, of course, reply appropriately and I will be forthcoming about my father's treatment here.

"I will also take the opportunity to talk about my aunt's need for care. The provision of social care is obviously a hot topic of debate at the moment though hardly within my own administrative brief. I expect you will receive a degree of media attention as a result."

He pauses for dramatic effect to ensure his message is being fully digested.

"Can you assure me you will review your confidentiality protocols immediately and ensure neither you nor your staff report any information concerning my father and aunt other than we, the family, have entrusted them both to your care, have always been deeply concerned about their long term health and safety, and that we adhere to the clinical advice you have given regarding their ongoing welfare.

"Finally, neither my father or aunt have any relatives or friends who are likely to visit. If anyone tries to make an appointment to see them treat it as suspicious and contact me immediately. Now, let's go and see my father."

The Politician doesn't really wish to spend any time with his father but recognises the need to waste an hour of his precious time with the senile old reprobate to assure the director that there is some degree of familial interest in his ongoing welfare. He will also be able to use today's personal visitation during tomorrow's morning media interviews when the inevitable question 'when was the last time you saw your father?' will, without doubt, be raised - as always, attention to the finer details.

The director gets up from his desk - "of course - let me take you up to his room.

The director opens the office door and ushers the Politician out into the corridor where they walk towards the residents lift. They take the lift to the first floor where they proceed down a corridor almost identical to the one leading to the director's office, with the thick beige woollen carpet and the high-quality light magnolia paint punctuated with original works of second rate art.

They approach a door at the end of the corridor. The director knocks on this door and without waiting for a response uses a pass key to secure entry. They walk in - the Politician sees the father sat slumped in a chair with a newspaper opened on his lap. There is a side table with a glass of water on it.

The father has been allocated a large ensuite bedroom on the first floor. It also has a window overlooking the gardens. However, as with all residents' rooms, this window has been secured and is incapable of being opened more than a couple of inches. This precautionary measure is designed to prevent the escape or accidental departure of the inmate.

The room has a tall ceiling and is painted in the same high quality light magnolia paint obviously used throughout the whole of the building. As a long term resident the father has been allowed to furnish the room with some of his treasured belongings. His vintage Edwardian wardrobe, a Victorian dresser, some original paintings of dubious origin, and various china ornaments collected over the years, adorn the interior.

The director turns to the Politician. "I will leave you with him. Any problems just press the call button on the wall near his chair and we will respond."

"Oh I doubt there will be any problems - do you pops?"

The director turns around, walks back through the door and down the corridor.

The father considers the person stood in front of him. He looks strangely familiar.

"Do I know you?" He asks.

The Politician scans the room in search of a chair. He sees one on the other side of the room and walks over, picks it up, walks back over to the father places it in front of him, sits down, and smiles -

"Of course you do. I just called you pops didn't I. It is me, your ever dutiful loving son. I have come to visit and see how you are doing."

****

Sixty-seven minutes after entering the building he walks out of the entrance having left the director in the lobby with strict instructions there should be a welcoming committee waiting outside the entrance on his return with their new guest. He looks around for his little security minder who is nowhere to be seen. He walks over to the car and finds the man twenty yards away behind a bush puffing away on a vape.

"You were supposed to drive the car over as soon as I came out of the building like a good little chauffeur. People are watching all the time and we need to create the appropriate impression. Now what have I told you about the need to be ready at the drop of a needle. I seem to recall we had a similar conversation this morning. I expect efficiency at all times, otherwise you are no use to me - you know what I mean.

"Now come on - do your duties properly. We are going to drive into the little town next door, pay a little visit to the old coach house hotel on the high street. I am about to introduce myself to my long-lost aunt who is in need of our assistance. We will be bringing her back here with all her belongings. She has a room at the hotel so while I am talking to her you will need to speak to reception, explain who we are, and go and fetch the luggage. You can tell reception I will be paying her bill. I don't expect there will be any difficulty in that. You will need to go in before me and locate her. She will probably be in the bar. Make sure there is no-one else there. If there are people around find a meeting room or somewhere similar where I can converse with her in private - no prying eyes or curious ears. Come along then, pass me the key fob - I'm driving."

They arrive at the dreary little market town twenty-three minutes later and pull up into a car park just behind the high street, close to the old coach house hotel. The Politician gets out of the car and looks around him - he can't understand how anyone would want to live in such a dismal environment - yet people did, the very sort of people he will need to vote for him at the next election. He smells the air and catches the unmistakeable whiff of cannabis. He looks around and sees a group of disaffected teenagers sitting under a shelter on the far side of the car park smoking, drinking, and vaping.

He turns away and ignores them - he has no time for such dull-witted malcontents - they are insignificant, just as people of his age and social standing are of no consequence to them. This particular brand of youth will always be dissatisfied and no government will ever change the fact - let history attest to that little reality. Let them enjoy themselves whilst they can. Their future is relatively predictable - some mundane job with no career prospects, marriage, children like themselves, who will one day take up residency under the same shelter to smoke dope, drink cheap cider and vape. He happily accedes to the simple truth that the country needs them as much as anyone else - to do all the tedious low paid jobs required to keep the economy moving. It is just pointless wasting tax monies on trying to improve their lot when they are congenitally disinterested in everyday life beyond themselves.

The little security minder gets out of the car and seems to be waiting to receive his instructions. The Politician sighs impatiently.

"You know what to do, I've already explained it to you. Now go across to the hotel and find where she is. As I said she is most probably in the bar. Don't frighten her - don't even talk to her. Come back and tell me the lie of the land."

After a few minutes the little security minder returns.

"As you thought she is in the bar. There is no-one else with her and no-one else in the lounge. There is only one person on duty looking after the reception and the bar. You should be able to go in and talk to her without being disturbed. At this time of day I don't think there will be any more customers coming in. I will divert the receptionist and explain you are the woman's nephew who has come collect and move her into a new home. I will also get him take me up to her room so I can collect her belongings. Do you want me to settle the bill so you don't have to engage with the receptionist. You can reimburse me when I put in my expenses."

"Good god man. You are thinking strategically for a change. Yes - do that. However, you will be paying by cash." He pauses for a moment and removes a wallet from his jacket pocket, opens it and removes a wad of twenty-pound notes. "There's seven hundred pounds here, it shouldn't be any more than that. Get a proper bill and receipt and make sure to give me back the change."

They walk across the road and into the hotel. His little security minder wanders over to reception and rings the bell. The Politician walks across the floor focussing intently on the entrance to the bar, ignoring anything coming within his peripheral vision. He enters the bar and sees a woman sat on a stool at a table close to a small open fire. She appears to be asleep or deep in thought as her eyes are closed. There is an old plastic supermarket bag for life placed next to her. He recognises the woman - there is a family likeness. He walks over as she suddenly jolts awake and looks up at him. He looks down and smiles.

"Hello aunt."

She looks at him quizzically.

"Do I know you......?" She asks.

"Of course you do - didn't I just call you aunt? Say hello to your loving nephew." He smiles.

****

The following day, having successfully navigated his way through the mandatory early morning round of media interviews, it is time to takes his seat in front of the legendary septuagenarian host of the internationally renowned mid-morning chat show which is aired each weekday on national television.

After he is introduced he walks onto the stage to receive the rapturous cue driven applause from the audience. He pauses for a moment to acknowledge their acclamation, proceeds over to where the host is stood waiting for him, kisses her on the cheek, and sits down.

He has appeared on this show willingly on numerous occasions over the last six years and has become a popular guest with the regular viewers. As a result he has helped increase the old interviewer's approval ratings to such a level her employers have had no choice but to keep extending her contract and salary when they would probably have preferred to pension her off.

This is of no particular concern to him - it has always been obvious she finds him deeply attractive, who wouldn't. They both play the game, a little bit of surreptitious flirting on live television makes him appear infinitely more human than the majority of his colleagues. The questions asked on the show have never been too challenging and he continues to find he can morph any interview with this infatuated old crone into a party political broadcast for himself. Today will be no different.

There has been a ripple of laughter when he kissed her on the cheek, and she visibly blushed before sitting down. She gives him her best serious look, but before she can speak the Politician interrupts.

"You know you have interviewed me so many times over the years and I just want to say to your faithful audience of viewers how much I have grown to respect your show, the veracity of your interviewing style, and the professional approach you have towards your job. Personally, I think you truly are a treasure and a credit to your profession.

The interviewer blushes again and crosses her legs - oh he is such a gorgeous man, if only...

"Thank you secretary of state - obviously there is no need for me to formally introduce you to our audience again. Everyone knows who you are." She smiles at the Politician and the Politician smiles back amiably. "Now, regardless of your kind words, I have some very difficult questions today which I know the audience would like some honest replies to." She pauses to provide the serious look viewers at home will be expecting to see.

"Ask away. As you know I am more than happy to give full answers to all your questions without any obfuscation." He now takes on an expression similar to the one adopted by a top tennis professional on the waiting end of a serve. "The ball is in your court."

"Well Secretary of State it has been reported in the media your father has been placed in an expensive upmarket residential care home. Bearing in mind the parlous situation of social care provision in the country the deputy leader of the opposition has accused you of hypocrisy intimating you have only done so because the state provision is so poor."

"Hypocrisy, hypocrisy, hypocrisy. Anything the government does to better the lives of our citizens is decried as hypocrisy by an opposition who have no plans of their own to offer.

"I have a great deal of respect for the many people working within social care. Yes, they are doing a challenging job and yes, we are doing a great deal of work to improve the system. I could have placed my father in a social care home and got the state to pay for it - he is as entitled to these services as much as everyone else. But I ask you - my family have the resources to pay for his care. If we had used social provision what would I have been accused of then? Hypocrisy?" He pauses for a moment and turns to look directly into the television camera recording his response.

"My family should not really be a source for media gossip. They have a right to privacy which I have obviously had to forego because of my prominent role in government. Yet I will tell you now, so it does not become a source of malicious tittle tattle, we have recently had to place my ailing aunt in the same home - she is no longer capable of looking after herself and needs a level of care beyond that which the family is able to provide.

"Why are we paying her care? Simple, because I believe that where people have the financial resources available they should pay. There are many people using the social care system who have more than enough money to contribute - yet they don't - it is simply unfair. I am leading by example. Why would my family place any extra burden on the strained resources of the social care system when we can afford to pay." He turns away from the camera and fixes the interviewer in his gaze.

Oh, how masterful he is - she uncrosses her legs and brushes the left hand side of her cheek with the palm of her hand.

"So Secretary of State, what is the government doing about social care?"

"Well, there is no doubt the government inherited a system from the opposition which had been neglected for many years. As you said, it is in a parlous state. My colleague as secretary of state for social care has undertaken a review and has asked for proposals recommending how we can fix this situation once and for all. No-one should need to worry about how they are going to be looked after when they get older. I have seen the recommendations and believe a solution has been found which is fair to everyone. I can't say anything more than that for the moment - the proposals are currently being discussed in cabinet."

The interviewer crosses her legs again and leans forward slightly toward the Politician.

"Secretary of State - there have been some rumours concerning the prime minister's health and that he may be showing some signs of early onset dementia. There are also rumours that some of your colleagues are seeking to oust him from office. What is going on?"

The Secretary of State laughs out aloud.

"Total bunkum. Rest assured, only this morning I spoke to the prime minister and he seems to be totally fit and on top of the amazingly responsible job he has of leading the country. Yes, I have heard the rumours of back bench disaffection and that a few letters of no confidence may have been submitted to the executive party council - but it is ever thus, regardless of which party is in government - there is always an element of discontent. We are a broad church. If," he emphasises the word, "if there is any sort of conspiracy to remove the prime minister I am certainly not a party to it."

He turns to look directly at the camera -

"Let me say this to all of you - he is the politician the country voted for in the last election, gaining a more than healthy mandate to lead the country. He ran on a very full and positive manifesto which we are delivering successfully - he has my unconditional support and confidence. Let me be completely honest here, I would never ever go against the wishes of the electorate. It is a line I will not cross."

****

As the Politician leaves the television studio he is pleased with himself - all the finer details have been taken care of bar one. His brother-in-law - the bohemian writer and now journalist at the local city gazette. A Job has been offered and his mother has assured him his sister will ensure it is accepted.

Part 3 - The Journey towards Truth

'At which point between sleep and consciousness do you truly wake up?'

Some of your philosophers claim humanity has been granted freedom of will - the ability to choose and determine the actions required to live life within society. Indeed this belief is a fundamental tenet within many of the religions invented by your species.

Alas free will in this dimension is extremely difficult to develop, and the power to make any indeterministic decision, for many, remains merely an illusion. Most humans in your world live within a complicated system of reaction - the laws of cause and effect. We have witnessed many who claim to have free will yet commit the most grievous of sins when they react rather than respond to many a given situation - they are left behind to reflect on why they behaved in such a manner - some may feel guilt. Others, if they become truly aware of themselves, may experience remorse.

Can you escape the deterministic laws of cause and effect and retrieve your true destiny?

You live in a world of dreams. Everyone would like a bright and brilliant future. They live and identify with the delusions cascading in the forefront of their mind - they miss the magic of the present. Of course your dreams and desires are important but only when observed in the moment. Unfortunately, whilst most believe they are living in the present, in reality they are identifying with a future which does not exist or a past which is no longer relevant in the moment - they are asleep. So what is the truth of your situation?

When people talk of truth they are generally referring to the meaning they give their life during their current sojourn within this world. However, your living body has a limited span of time and at some point it will die. The journey towards truth has to include the reality of death, for the inevitable peregrination of life concludes with death - and no-one is aware of the time and place their bodily existence will be extinguished. Many individuals appear unwilling to accept the reality of their demise until it is upon them.

This is regardless of the fact that many will philosophise and develop a sincere faith about what occurs following death. Whether this is merely wishful thinking, a way in which to ameliorate the fear of death, would appear to be true for some but not for others.

So let us continue our discourse by exploring some of the beliefs people have regarding the truth of their life and death on this planet. What we will tell you is purely from the perspective of our witnessing over the aeons of time.

Firstly, let us conclude, however, that our existence as a repository of all your thoughts and actions demonstrates a certain form of immortality - the experience your life whilst you were biologically sentient lives on within us after the death of your physical body. Whilst this may appear to be a confirmation of faith for those who believe life after death exists solely within the memories of others - it is not.

Many have believed that each individual born into a human body is in possession of an embodied soul, an independent living source which continues to exist beyond the death of your existing mortal body in some form, or reborn into a new entity, the nature of which will be dependent on previous behaviour - whether it was good or evil.

Whether this is a truth we cannot answer for the reality lies beyond both your and our current experience of life.

What we do know as a certainty is that upon death your earthly body breaks down and returns to the chemical elements from which it was formed, predominantly oxygen, hydrogen, nitrogen, carbon, calcium, and phosphorus. Many consider this a miracle in itself and believe in nothing else.

Others believe in a final resurrection of the body at the conclusion of the apocalypse - the end of the world and the last judgement. Those who have been good will be sent to some form of paradise whilst those who have been evil will be dispatched to a correction centre, hell and damnation.

The reality of good and evil is a complex concept, especially as what is deemed evil at one time is considered good in another. To truly sin means to miss the mark - to stray from the line of the path set out for each individual.

From our perspective each individual has an inherent conception of what is good and evil - an instinctive reality they are born with and exists within. However, the majority lose their ability to listen to what is within them preferring to follow the 'norms' of the society in which they live. It is only immediately prior to death when some of them will consider whether or not their actions have been good.

We obviously have no experience of a future resurrection, nonetheless, we have witnessed the devout faith of all who believe in this - it is part of the collective consciousness from which we are formed.

In other beliefs some deny the validity of the body and seek to expunge its needs, believing an absence of feeling and control over their body will lead them closer to the source of all being. Whilst some sincerely believe they find the truth in this way, many become insane.

Others believe the desires of the body should be gratified for it only exists for a finite period of time. Sadly, the majority of these people cease to have an awareness of anything around them, they live in a permanent sleep, missing the mark of meaning.

Finally, there are those who choose to explore the human conditioning placed upon them through the constructs of society, trying to move forward along the line of the path given to them and experience a way of life beyond the habitual sleep in which they generally live.

Their aim is to rise beyond the laws of cause and effect and to take some form of responsibility for their life. Very few succeed, though some have managed to move toward the destiny they were allotted at birth - this is a rare achievement. The majority, however, only wallow in the pain created through their own awakened observations of a personal inability to act. The others observe their condition and move on.

We have witnessed, and we will continue to do so, the death of every person who has lived on this peculiar little planet we share together.

Some deaths are sudden, unexpected, and comes as a surprise to the victim who has little time to contemplate what is occurring to them. Others, aware of their forthcoming demise fight to their very last breath ignoring the futility of their struggle to cling onto mortality.

Then there are those who embrace their death as a release from the pain they experience in the world - they may even bring about the termination of their own living body.

The rarest however, are the persons who accept the inevitability of their death in the knowledge of contentment that they instinctively and consciously led a selfless and good life. To share in the presence of such people, even for a moment, is both a gift and a blessing.

Chapter 7 - The Chief Executive

'The truth rarely remains
in one place long enough to be found.
Be aware of where you seek it
for time can only be experienced in the moment.'

It has been a particularly long and challenging day - one which the Chief Executive would have preferred not to have experienced. Nevertheless, it is his duty to accept the rough with the smooth. He sighed - he hadn't realised it would be so easy to get the board of RLE Services PLC to propose serving notice on the Chairman - the level of antagonism held against the man was more far-reaching than he had anticipated.

An emergency meeting of shareholders has been convened and it is unlikely his old friend and mentor will be able to do much to save his job - even if he actually desires to do so. However, the Chairman and his stepsisters will remain major shareholders of the company - what will they do? Will they sell their shares and retire gracefully from the scene, or will they try to fight for control of the business? The board has proposed to make an offer to buy them out individually.

Too many internal politics - too many balls in the air waiting to be caught. Nevertheless, it is his duty to steer the company in a straight line down the path of ever-increasing growth in order to maintain competitive advantage and profitability.

There is absolutely no doubt in his mind that unless they dealt with what many on the board perceive to be a problem in the management of the business, the company's public sector contracts would be at risk. The Secretary of State had implied as much in their early morning meeting a week ago. Of course he had not relayed the content of the meeting to the board, he was more than aware this would create an additional angst far more difficult to contain. Instead he has to be seen as the instigator of the Chairman's downfall - the traitor wielding the knife.

You don't get to his level of responsibility without a little of the killer instinct instilled within your DNA - a successful business, such as RLE Services PLC has risen to be, requires professionals accomplished in the game, people who can safely deal with the daily cut and thrust of commercial realpolitik.

His mentor, the Chairman, had always seemed able to raise himself above the grimy affray of duplicitous scheming - possibly because he relied on others, like the Chief Executive, to do all the dirty work for him.

Yet the Chairman is clearly out of touch - detached from how the corporation had developed since the merger with ROC Services PLC and incapable of acknowledging the business's commercial needs. RLE was never going to remain the same idealistic organisation envisaged by the Chairman and his guardian when it was originally founded.

As far as the Chief Executive is concerned the future of RLE Services PLC belongs to him - the Chairman belongs to the past together with all the utopian baggage he has collected on the journey.

The board have offered him the mantle of interim chairman until a suitable replacement can be found. He has accepted their proposal and, subject to the agreement of the shareholders, he will undertake both the duties of chairman and chief executive concurrently.

On one level he is extremely pleased with himself and how he has just managed to navigate so successfully around the complexity of the 'issue' facing the business.

On another level he feels like a Judas betraying his master and is a deeply disturbed about the chain of events he has set in motion.

Previously he would have discussed his conflicting emotions with either his mentor or wife in an endeavour to make some sort of sense out of them. However, neither of these redoubtable sources of wisdom are available to him anymore.

He is no longer on speaking terms with his ex-spouse, and, even if he had the effrontery to contact to his old mentor, no-one is quite sure where he is or what he is currently up to - the Chairman appears to have vanished off the face of the earth. Another small problem which he will have to deal with as they are desperately trying to keep tabs on him...

The Chief Executive is exhausted by it all - he desperately needs to relax. A quiet night listening to some soothing music is the order of the day.

It is dark when he pulls up and parks his car next to the house he now calls home. He stops the engine and reaches over across the passenger seat to retrieve a small bag of groceries and his briefcase. Stepping out he walks slowly through the wicket gate across the stone pathway toward the front door of his cottage.

He had moved into the detached cottage a few weeks before, following the finalisation of his divorce. He paid cash for the property, which he understood had been empty and languishing on the market for the previous two years.

The cottage was pretty and situated on the edge of a village, at the side of a country lane leading into the small forest much beloved by local dog walkers. It had been recently renovated, with a new kitchen and bathroom, did not require redecorating, and was, as the estate agent described it to him, ready to 'go'. With four bedrooms there was space for a home office and a few occasional guests.

Set within the middle of a large garden he had fantasies about entertaining his friends there at weekends. The first of such events is due this very weekend, a group of his university alumni, men he has continued to hang out with over the years, are joining him for a housewarming party. No women have been invited - he feels this would be inappropriate following his recent divorce - just a group of lads with a connoiseurial appreciation of fine wines, who enjoy playing sport together and undertaking a little cross trail bike riding in the country.

As he walks toward the door he pauses; there is a strange flickering light coming through the porch window. He can't remember leaving a light on - it wasn't the sort of thing he would do - he was quite particular about conserving energy. He blinks and looks again - no, he must have been mistaken - there is no light.

He turns around and looks towards his car - he presses the key fob to just check he has actually locked it. As he turns back, he can see the flickering light again. It is the glimmering glow of a fire, one that is burning inside his cottage.

Feeling a rising surge of panic he rushes to the door, places his briefcase and bag of groceries at the side of the porch, and retrieves the door keys from his pocket. He hurriedly places them into the lock and is about to turn the key when he suddenly realises the door is unlocked. "No," he thinks to himself, "I definitely locked up this morning."

He picks up his brief case and bag of groceries and enters the hallway. Except this is not his hallway. The area he observes appears to be of the same size and dimension, but this space is dark and dingy with a burning fire set within what appears to be an old-fashioned integral cooking range with a battered copper kettle of water boiling on top of it. There is a wooden table placed in front of the range, and, most disconcertingly, three people sat on chairs warming themselves - a man, a woman, and a teenage boy.

In his tiredness he had obviously walked into the wrong house - how could he have been so stupid?! He turns to walk out, hoping he hasn't been noticed. As he opens the door, he finds himself looking out at his car, which is parked by his wicket gate, next to his garden. In his confusion he stumbles and falls onto the flag stone floor of the porch.

The noise rouses the residents of the table who all turn to look at him. The man stands up from his chair and turns to the woman.

"Well Mother, it appears we have an uninvited guest barging into our home - should we invite him in?"

Well Husband, look how he's dressed, seems a bit of a toff to me - what say you son?"

"I reckon he's dressed a bit of a Mary-Anne myself, Ma. The old man next door is more his type. Maybe we should ask him why he's a trespassing inside our home." The three of them look toward the trespasser in askance.

The trespasser is now staring at the three people in front of him in disbelief. They are scruffily dressed and appear, from the soil stains on their clothes, to have been working in the garden - not his garden surely? The woman is wearing a simple wool dress with a white collar. Her hair, dirty blond going grey, is placed in a bun on top of her head. The man and boy are clothed in identical woollen trousers and a smock shirt, the man is also wearing an apron.

"What on earth are you doing in my house?" the trespasser manages finally to stutter having struggled to find something appropriate to say.

The three occupants look at him quizzically before bursting into peals of laughter.

"My house, Mother, did you hear that? Why sir, it's not even our house, but it is our home. We are tenants here working for the miserly old landlord who lives next door. Tis been in his family for generations. Is it him you've come to see? Well, you're in the wrong house, his is next door - the door just up along the path. Easy mistake to make, he never lights a candle let alone a fire."

The man returns to his seat still laughing until he sees the trespasser has not moved.

"What yer waiting for - get out of our home. You and your sort aren't welcome here."

The Chief Executive remains nonplussed until it dawns on him - he is on the receiving end of an elaborate practical joke set up by his friends - possibly an advance housewarming prank. He is not in the mood - especially not today.

"Look here," he replies wearily, "I don't know what you're doing here - I bought this property a couple of months ago. It's my house. I don't know how you managed to set this up. There is no house next door - this is just an old detached renovated cottage. There is no man living next door. I am really tired. I have had an especially bad day at the office. Let me turn on the light and maybe we could have a drink together - I have some wine cooling in the fridge. Then you can tell me who put you up to this (I think I know by the way) and then you can explain how you managed to get in - quite impressive really, obviously it took some planning."

The Chief Executive turns to the door, finds the light switch and presses it down. There is a sudden flood of light. He looks around - the occupants have gone, there is no table, no fire, and no cooking range. He is stood in the entrance hall of the cottage clutching his briefcase and a bag of groceries.

It was a little later after he had settled down with a recuperative gin and tonic when he finally managed to make sense of what had happened. Of course - he was extremely tired from having to direct an exceedingly complicated combination of operational processes.

The meeting with the board of directors earlier that day had been a potential minefield stretching his intellectual and emotional capabilities to the limit. Was he now suffering from some form of extreme stress psychosis and exhaustion? Well, he reasoned, it would explain the hypnagogic hallucination.

He had studied psychology as part of his law degree and had read case histories where people suffering from extreme stress occasionally experienced waking dreams. He laughs at himself - surely he wouldn't be prone to such an episode.

Nevertheless, he will accept this evening's little episode as a warning to take more care of his health; he was overworked and under a fair degree of emotional pressure, the divorce had taken its toll on him and he had just moved house – both considered highly stressful situations. He would take it easy tomorrow and work from home, recuperate and regain a hold over himself mentally.

A few hours later, having emailed his office to notify them of his decision, he walks upstairs to his bedroom. With an immense sense of relief he lies down on his bed fully dressed, looks up to the ceiling and, unintentionally, falls into a deep sleep.

Suddenly he awakes, pulled out of his slumber with a shock - disorientated - there is a light flickering in the corner of the room next to the door and the shape of three people inside his bedroom.

In an instance he sees the knife hovering above his eyes, held by the same man who had been downstairs earlier.

"Ah, look at him now Mother - wide awake and not yet ready to die. So you skin-flinting bastard you would try and evict us from our home would you - well now I'm about to evict you from life."

He rolls over sideways and falls to the floor just as the knife enters the pillow where his head had just been. He screams out in alarm as the man raises the knife again. He reaches toward his bed side light and finds the switch.

The room is filled with light - he is alone. He checks the pillow - there are no knife marks. He lies back on his bed breathing heavily listening carefully as to whether or not the assailants are nearby.

He gets up slowly from his bed and looks around for a suitable object he could use to defend himself with. He picks up a dresser chair opens the door and walks into the corridor holding the back of the chair with the legs pointing forward.

He switches on the light - there is no-one there or any sign of anyone having been in the corridor. He checks each of the upstairs rooms and the bathroom - again, there is no sign of any intrusion.

He walks slowly down the stairs and investigates the hall, kitchen, dining room, and lounge - no sign of any intruders. It must have been nightmare - yet it had seemed so real. He laughs at himself - how could any of it really have happened. Yes, it was probably his subconscious processing the residual guilt he was feeling about his old mentor and friend.

Nevertheless, when he returns to his bed he leaves all the upstairs lights on and then finally, after an hour or so, he falls into an uneasy sleep...

The following morning he wakes up much later than normal. The sun is shining bright through the trees making patterns of leaves flicker over his duvet. He lies in his bed for a little while luxuriating in the warm dappling light before eventually realising he should get up and commence the day. Although he is working from home there is still plenty he needs to achieve.

He gets out of bed, walks down the corridor to the bathroom, has a quick shower, returns to his bedroom where he gets dressed in his favoured casual attire - a pair Italian design camel-coloured chinos and a single fitted linen shirt.

It is 8.53 am when he finally arrives downstairs in his kitchen, where he proceeds to brew up some fresh coffee in an old battered copper cafetière, fills a cast iron sauce pan with some unpasteurised raw milk and places it on the boiling plate of his range cooker. Finally, he puts three slices of wholemeal bread in the toaster.

He sits down on an oaken bar stool at his large black marble kitchen island awaiting for the bread to metamorphose into toast, and falls into a day dream - "what a crazy unbelievable night that was..."

He is jolted back into reality - someone is knocking on the front door - he is not expecting any visitors and instantly he becomes anxious. He is still feeling a tad spooked from the previous day's nightmares.

He stops for a moment, considers his predicament, and then laughs ruefully to himself - he is being silly. He gets up from his stool, walks over to the cooking range and moves the milk pan onto the simmering plate, wanders down the passageway to the entrance hall and opens the front door.

He is greeted by a man of an indeterminable older age wearing a threadbare yet clean black cassock.

"Good morning neighbour. I live in the bungalow just down the lane from you. I thought I would come over, introduce myself and welcome you to our select little enclave. I saw your car parked outside the gate so considered today was probably a good a time as any. I also noticed all your upstairs lights were on all last night, so I just wanted to check you were ok. I have left my bike fastened to the fence behind your car if that is alright with you."

The Chief Executive scrutinises the man's apparel is not sure how to respond. The old man in the cassock is standing in front of him obviously anticipating some form of dialogue - at the moment he really isn't in the mood to exchange pleasantries. Nevertheless... it would not do to upset a neighbour so soon after moving in, especially if that neighbour is a man of the cloth.

"Are you the parish priest?" Enquires the Chief Executive.

The man in the cassock looks confused for a moment and then laughs. "Oh no - I wouldn't be seen dead in one of their churches. Wearing a cassock is just an old habit of mine. I have never really taken to 'civvy' clothes - can't really see myself in jeans somehow."

"Do I know you? There seems something familiar about you. Have we met?"

The old man smiles - a friendly and quite jovial smile.

"No, we have not met before, but to be quite frank and honest our paths have crossed in the past, albeit not in person. There was some correspondence between us regarding the psychometric assessment tool you were developing. At the time you were the company secretary and head of legal services at RLE Incorporated Limited. I had recently been retired as the Pastor from the Church of Universal Values - your company did some research relating to your psychometric assessment with my successor. Anyway, it is of no import to me now."

The Chief Executive immediately becomes defensive. Of course he now recognises the old man with the cassock - they had kept a picture of him in the security file just in case he turned up at head office. Back then the man had become a comprehensive pain in the proverbial with all his letters of complaint, online postings, and sham reviews of the company's renowned psychometric assessment tool - he had challenged the veracity and undermined the statistical research supporting its development.

Eventually the company had no recourse but to threaten him with legal action. They never heard from him again. At the time he had assumed the matter was resolved - cosily put to bed out of sight and mind. His response to the old man is terse.

"If you have come to talk about RLE company business with me you will need to contact our head office and arrange a meeting.

"If you are still harking on about our psychometric assessment tool I seem to recall we made it very clear to you at the time we would take legal action against you for defamation if you continued to cast negative aspersions over its development and use.

"I am working from home today, I am really busy, and this is not an appropriate time or place to resurrect issues which were resolved some time ago. Thank you for coming around to see me. I am sure we will bump into each again but for the moment I don't have the time to talk to you..."

The Chief Executive turns and is about shut the door when he notices the old man in the cassock has not moved. He remains obstinately stood in the porch staring fixedly at him - he is no longer wearing a jovial smile, instead his face appears to be in conflict with itself, trying to suppress a degree of irritation.

Nonetheless, when he does continue speaking his voice still manages to maintain what are generally considered to be the elemental tones of affability.

"You don't appear to have heard me correctly. My sole intention here is to introduce myself and be neighbourly. The affairs of your business are no longer any concern of mine and I have absolutely no desire to resurrect issues from the past in order to have an argument with you on your doorstep.

"We are neighbours and in my tradition we believe those people who live in close vicinity to each other should show a degree of friendly respect."

He pauses, smiles again, and can't resist a little contrariness. He has a good idea how to get the Chief Executive's attention - a little teasing is in order. He continues...

"Anyway, I have come to realise it is no longer any of my business what you do with your psychometric assessment. Your chairman enlightened me on that point when I met with him recently."

He pauses and ascertains he has the Chief Executive's attention.

"Or should I be referring to him as your ex-chairman - he does seem to be making the most of his sabbatical."

He registers the sudden look of shock on the Chief Executive's face. Yes, the last comment was probably inappropriate.

"No matter, the affairs of your business, as I said before, are no longer any concern of mine - today or tomorrow."

The old man in the cassock is more than aware he has piqued the Chief Executive's curiosity. Indeed the Chief Executive's thought processes have been more than readily stimulated - what on earth had the Chairman been thinking of reaching out to this wily old man?

Whilst he would prefer the old man with the cassock to leave him alone and return from whence he came, realistically he has no choice, it is his duty to the company to try and obtain as much information as possible concerning the Chairman's current whereabouts and state of mind.

The old man in the cassock is more than aware this is exactly what the Chief Executive is contemplating - it is what he intended. The Chief Executive breaks the ensuing silent impasse.

"Sorry - I didn't mean to appear rude. I wasn't expecting any visitors this morning. It's very thoughtful of you to come and check up on me - very neighbourly.

"I must confess I did have a somewhat sleepless night. Work has been a little stressful of late and I may have overdone it. Anyway, as a result, I had a rather unpleasant dream so I do apologise if I came across a little tetchy.

"It also came as a bit of a surprise when I realised who you were - what a strange coincidence. Anyway you're quite right, whatever happened in the past shouldn't impact upon our relationship now."

He pauses before proceeding cautiously with his line of careful inquisition.

"So, you met our chairman recently?.. May I ask how he was?.. We haven't heard from him for a little while?... He was my mentor and friend, and I am feeling a little concerned about his welfare and current state of mind. Do you know where he is at the moment? We need to contact him? Also, do you mind if I ask why he wanted to meet you?"

The old man in the cassock listens amiably to what the Chief Executive has to say before responding

"I notice you said he was your mentor and friend. Is the past tense intentional. Anyway, this is not a conversation for the doorstep. I can see you are concerned. Would you care to invite me in and I will tell you what I know?"

He frowns and holds the Chief Executive within his eyes until he receives an appropriate response.

"Of course you may come in." He endeavours to say these words without them sounding too trenchant. "I've just made a pot of coffee and I have some toast on the go - would you care to join me?"

The old man in the cassock acquiesces and follows the Chief Executive through the front door, down the entrance hall and into the kitchen where he is invited to take a seat on one of the stools positioned next to the kitchen island.

The Chief Executive walks over to a Welsh dresser situated to the left-hand side of the cooking range and brings out two plates, pottery mugs, a couple of knives and teaspoons. These he places upon the island, one set in front of the old man, and the other set opposite to the visitor.

He proceeds over to the fridge where he takes out a butter dish together with a jar of apricot jam, these he positions onto the centre of the island between the plates and pottery mugs. He reaches over to the toaster and removes two pieces of the wholemeal toast and deposits a piece on each plate, one of which he sets down in front of the old man.

He pores the coffee from the battered copper cafetière into the pottery mugs, removes the saucepan containing the unpasteurised milk from the simmering plate on the range, and proffers the old man a little to go with his coffee. The old man with the cassock declines the offer with a wave of his hand. They fall into an uncomfortable tense silence.

The Chief Executive feels the discomfort intensely. He considers the old man. He appears to be meditating over his mug of coffee which he is currently holding between both hands.

Is he creating the palpable sense of tension enveloping the atmosphere on purpose? He catches hold of the thought - don't be so stupid, of course he's not. He smiles at his own stupidity.

The old man in the cassock notices and smiles back deciding to release the strained atmosphere between them and break the hold of the silence. He places his mug of coffee down onto the Island in front of him.

"I understand your concern, but you really have nothing to worry about - there is no need to be defensive. In all honesty I had no ulterior motive for coming to see you other than introduce myself as your neighbour. Of course I was interested in meeting you in person but as I said your business is no longer any concern of mine. However, I will answer the questions you raised with me at the door.

"I saw your Chairman a couple of weeks ago at the old coach house hotel situated in the high street of our neighbouring market town. He arranged to meet me to discuss certain details regarding the death of his aunt.

"Whilst I was Pastor at the Church of Universal Values she was a respected member of the congregation and became a valued friend and confidante of mine throughout the latter years of my ministry. In a letter she requested that he should deliver her ashes to an old ashram she had once stayed at in India and for the ashes to be sprinkled over the river Ganges from the bank of the temple next door.

"He was seeking my advice concerning his journey. I happen to know the Guru of the ashram and agreed to write a letter of introduction." The old man in the cassock looks thoughtful for a moment.

"As far as his welfare and state of mind is concerned I have to say he looked well enough - though he also seemed slightly lost. He no longer has the personae of being the chairman of an internationally acclaimed organisation as an emotional support to fall back upon and so his life is naturally feeling quite empty. He is trying to ascertain a new identity for himself. He also seems to be suffering a degree of remorse over some of the decisions he made in the past regarding his business. His sabbatical has given him the opportunity to become a truth-seeker."

He notices a sudden look of concern on the Chief Executive's face.

"There is no need to worry. Yes, he obviously wanted to discuss the provenance of your company's beloved psychometric assessment tool. And, to be honest, I was certainly more than prepared to berate him for his involvement in its development.

"However, the long and short of the matter is that, following a relatively brief discussion, I came to realise the futility of my obsession in pursuing the hoary old chestnut any further - your precocious tool has little in common with the symbolism behind the original it was developed from and has consequently developed a life of its own. I advised him to let go of his little baby and allow it to find its own way in the world - a new truth will arise from its use soon enough.

"I imagine my response to your old friend and mentor is probably not the one you would have expected from me.

"As to his current whereabouts, I would guess by now he has embarked on a journey to the Ashram in India and I doubt he will be returning to the loving fold of your organisation as Chairman any time soon. Now that is all I have to say on the matter - let us talk about something else."

The old man in the cassock barely pauses before continuing.

"I am so pleased to see this lovely old cottage occupied again. You know, many people when they move into a new home like to hear a little of the history surrounding the property they have purchased. I have become a bit of a local historian since I moved here. You seem the curious type, would you like to know a little more about your new home?"

The Chief Executive is thrown off balance by the conversation's sudden change in tack. He would like to discover more about the Chairman's longer-term intentions - and he believes the old man in the cassock knows a smidgeon more than he is letting on to; what did he mean when he said 'I doubt he will be returning as your Chairman'? This statement at least needs a little clarification.

Anyway, it is obvious for the moment the old man in the cassock is not prepared to divulge anything further for the moment. Maybe encouraging him to talk about something else will change the atmosphere enabling him to re-direct the conversation back towards the Chairman. Anyway, the old man is quite correct, he is interested in the history of his new home. He pauses for a moment.

"Yes, I would actually like to learn a little more about the cottage. All I know of its history is what the estate agent told me - the previous occupiers were getting older and decided to move into an apartment within a new build residential retirement lodge. They exchanged their property with the lodge developers. It remained empty for a couple of years until they eventually decided to renovate and bring it up to date in order to make it more attractive to any potential purchaser like myself."

The old man in the cassock smiles. "Ah yes. After I moved to the village I became quite close to the previous occupants, they were a lovely couple and had lived here for over forty years. It was a happy house full of children and laughter. Mind you prior to that the house had a bit of a chequered history.

"This property was not always a single dwelling, though you would be hard pushed to notice it now. Originally it was two cottages - a smaller one just about where your front door is, and a larger one roughly where your lounge and master bedroom are situated. Back in the 1870's both properties were owned by an old man called Silas Jones. He lived in the larger property and tenanted out the smaller dwelling to a family of itinerant labourers - William and Mary Tyler together with their son James.

"They lived there happily for some years, until one night they entered their landlord's house, stole into his bedroom, where William repeatedly stabbed the old man through the eyes and killed him.

"The murder got quite a lot of press coverage back in the day. Contrary to our perception of those times, the violent murder of a neighbour was a pretty rare occurrence.

"The Tylers' defence, a pretty thin one even by the standards of the day, was they had learnt old Silas was about to make them homeless - evict them. They claimed that on the night of the murder, whilst sat in their kitchen, a strange man barged into their home claiming they were in his house and should leave immediately. Evidently, he was well spoken with a strange accent, wearing smart though rather peculiarly styled clothes. Probably the strangest part of the story as it was reported at the time was the conviction with which they told the lie, for regardless of all the publicity the case received, no-one ever found out who the man was...

"I have seen the articles and a picture of the man drawn up according to the description they gave - I have to say now we have met it bears an uncanny resemblance to you. I wonder, were they telling the truth?" He sees the look of horror on the Chief Executives face and laughs, "I am only joking, unless of course you know anything different."

The blood has drained from the Chief Executive's face. The old man notices and quickly guesses what his host's unpleasant dream was from the night before. He picks up his mug of coffee and sips it pensively. He starts to speak slowly and very carefully.

"Am I right in guessing your unpleasant dream from last night bears an uncanny resemblance to the story I just told you?"

The Chief Executive nods silently in the affirmative. The old man in the cassock continues.

"I was not intending to say anything about the symbol which formed the basis of your company's psychometric assessment, but I would like to explain part of its meaning from the tradition I follow. I believe you will find it helpful in making sense of what you are currently experiencing.

"Some elements of your company's exposition of its symbolism are relatively accurate. However, the interpretation misses some of the finer details of its explication which results in a static rather than fluid model of life, moving it away from its original and intended esoteric purpose.

"So, for example, whilst the cross in the centre does indeed create four quadrants relating to knowledge, creativity, labour and service, the beams creating the cross relate to aspects of how we experience time - this is not considered within your model. The upright beam represents time in eternity - a different dimension which we cannot normally experience. The lateral beam represents time as we generally experience it - from the past to the future. The centre where both lines cross represents time as we can live it - in the present moment with an awareness and the ability to respond to our external needs.

"If we live outside the awareness of the centre, as most of us do, we are asleep dreaming of a past or fantasising over a future which does not exist.

Occasionally, especially if we are tired and overtaxed by our work, we may lose ourselves totally within the line. In such a situation who knows where we go and what may occur when we fall beyond the confines of our ordinary daily reality. There are more dimensions existing in the universe than we experience in our ordinary life on earth – the dimension of time, as you probably know, is an incredibly complicated subject.

"I am aware you may be considering whether or not your house is haunted by the grim actuality of its past history. I can assure it is not. It's all a question of time..."

He pauses momentarily and glances at his watch.

"Talking of which I need to leave. There are matters at home I need to attend to. However, before I go, I would like to leave you with something to reflect on. There is no doubt you are extremely successful at what you do - I respect this fully. I can also sense you are a good man at heart with an intuitive understanding of what is correct and proper behaviour. It is also fairly obvious to an outside observer you are physically and mentally fatigued from your daily labours. Possibly you should also contemplate taking a sabbatical from your worldly travails and meditate on the direction your life is taking..."

Chapter 8 - The Evangelist

'The absence of Truth does not preclude its existence
It is of a finer energy most struggle to perceive.'

In our previous tales we have several times made mention of a coffee shop situated in the High Street of our favourite and somewhat overpopulated city. It is one of the typically franchised chains found invariably in towns and cities all over the country. Since we last made reference of it there has been a transfer of corporate ownership.

Consequently, the café has just received the inevitable brand makeover. The chairs and tables have been replaced along with the label of coffee being served. Likewise, the menu has been revamped to cater for the more current tastes favoured by the middling class of clientele who continue to frequent it. On offer there is now three grain muesli, crushed avocado salad with mixed seeds, humous platters, et al. Naturally the mandatory bacon and sausage baps, tuna melts, ham and cheese sandwiches still retain their unique placement within the fridge.

In reality the coffee shop is not particularly different from how it was before. Whilst the chairs and tables are new, they are still positioned in the same situation as their predecessors. And the three bifold glass doors still allow both a view over the river and access to the patio kitted out with the original and increasingly aged plastic rattan settees surrounded by low level wooden coffee tables. As today is a subsumed under dark grey clouds with a continuous rain pouring incessantly down on the river, no customers have chosen to sit outside.

Every time the evangelist returns to the city she always finds herself in this particular coffee shop - for some reason she finds it comfortably familiar, providing a space in which she can reflect on her life before moving on to somewhere else. She will always sit at the same table facing the door - she never sits with her back to the door for this makes her feel insecure. If someone else is sat in her seat when she comes in she will wait until the table is vacated before ordering her latte with a double shot of coffee. From this position she can view everyone who enters if she chooses to - she likes people watching, keeping an eye out for anyone who may succumb to her charms. Today she is most certainly in need of some inspiration for she hasn't got a clue as to what she should do next.

The evangelist is feeling extremely irritable and vexatious - more so than usual. And although she is becoming increasingly aware she has probably nurtured a degree of anger all her life, the reason for this is simple - nothing ever seems to run smoothly for her. All her desires and dreams for an enjoyable existence are thwarted by people around her who do not comprehend the meaning of her existence.

This is the first time she has returned to the city since her divorce over seven years ago. She had concluded, somewhat correctly, she should lie low for a while having managed to upset a large number of people during the course of her last residency. During that period she had been pastor of the Church of Universal Values, been discharged from the post, married the then business development director of RLE Incorporated Limited, and divorced him a mere 24 months later just prior to the company merger with ROC Services PLC.

Maybe if she had allowed the marriage to survive just a little while longer she would have exited the tedious connubial arrangement with a slightly more agreeable financial settlement.

Within the peculiarly warped benefit of her hindsight, she considers the fault for the whole unfortunate chain of events lies with the church elders. It was they who had initiated the unfortunate contiguity which eventually culminated in her divorce.

Her husband, a man significantly older than her, had not initially been a problem. It was the church who had concocted the plethora of difficulties which became increasingly troublesome to disentangle herself from whilst endeavouring to pursue the bohemian lifestyle she preferred engage with. For some reason the elders felt she had defrauded the congregation of their spiritual inheritance and tried to abscond with the funds due to the church as a result of a little research she did on behalf of RLE Incorporated Limited.

She picks up the large coffee cup and holds it in both hands bringing it up to the nose so she can smell the aroma. She sighs, 'at the end of the day it's all about money, I needed it, they didn't.'

In her own mind she didn't misappropriate anything from the church, she simply deciphered some musty old documents held in the church archives concerning the esoteric meaning of the old cross suspended above the altar of the Church of Universal Values and directly invoiced RLE Incorporated Limited for the privilege of her consultancy.

Nevertheless, whilst the elders had agreed to her doing the work, they had stipulated it was to be invoiced to the company through the church accounts - it was purely an administrative oversight on her part which would have been easily rectified if they hadn't removed her from her post.

She chooses to ignore the fact it was she who had actually absconded herself from the post before the elders had the chance to dismiss her for gross misconduct. On the same day she concluded her research she had been discovered asleep completely intoxicated in a pool of her own vomit and urine on a pew in front of the altar of the church. After being returned to the manse and put to bed by the church secretary, she awoke the following morning with the realisation she was in serious trouble and would more than likely be dismissed from her post.

She decided to pre-empt the church elders by arranging an immediate meeting with the business development director of RLE Incorporated Limited – the man who had originally approached her and the church to discover more about the origins of an image they were using as their company logo, a symbol which just happened to be a facsimile of the cross hanging above the church's altar.

She sent him a text message saying she would like to share her research findings with him in person that very day. She explained that because of some sensitivities with the church elders she did not want to meet him at the church but at the coffee shop in the city centre. She believed he would be excited by her findings as it appeared the logical interpretation of their logo provided a model of human nature which could be incorporated within the company's existing training models - in fact it could potentially be developed into a psychometric assessment which might positively impact the whole nature of how people lived and worked with each other.

He took the bait she had thrown out to him – hook line and sinker.

They met a couple of hours later in the city centre coffee shop she is now currently sat in. It was then she apprised him of the lachrymose state of her current living situation, i.e. she had had no alternative but to leave the church's employment with immediate effect (because the elders had never appreciated her brilliance) and consequently was now homeless and unemployed and needed somewhere to stay for a while. Using the research as an inducement, he was seduced by her beauty and personal charms and persuaded to take her into his home - she was after all a minister of religion and hardly likely to abuse him.

She handed over her thesis and issued the invoice to the company for her work a few days later after having signed a contract with them, drawn up by the director of business development, stating that the intellectual rights to whatever she had discerned within the research belonged solely to her and that she was now transferring all such rights to RLE Incorporated Limited. She considered the fee she would eventually receive in compensation for her work would be equivalent to the severance pay she must surely have been entitled to from the church following her dismissal. She married the director of business development a couple of months later.

There is no doubt the fantastical conclusion she expounded from her study of the archives was a work of genius - her mind operates at its creative intuitive best with the help of a few drugs and several glasses of wine - the church's reaction to her minor misdemeanour was an overreaction to the essential needs of her imagination.

Having said that, and in all due fairness to the elders, the discovery of her being completely inebriated in front of the church altar was actually the coup de grace, they had already been considering her dismissal - she had failed to meet any of the performance targets set for her, and the church congregation had begun to find her personal theology not particularly flavoursome.

RLE Incorporated Limited used the dénouement of her research for the development of the Symbolic Psychometric Personality Assessment™ later known simply as SPPA™. She had no idea how successful the psychological tool would become and that it would be employed on an international basis by governments and businesses all over the civilised world.

If only she had possessed the foresight to realise just how fruitful the product of her labour would turn out to be she would have negotiated ongoing royalties in recompense for the brilliance of her achievement.

Whatever... In the event it probably wouldn't have made any difference to the concatenation which ultimately led to her current predicament.

It was several months later before the church managed finally to uncover the truth of what had occurred on their watch - at the time their errant pastor appeared to have fallen off the face of the earth - no-one knew where she was. Eventually the penny dropped when the treasurer of the church decided to follow up on the research project with RLE Incorporated Limited.

He was extremely surprised to learn it had been completed and signed off - an invoice for the work undertaken had been settled and they were extremely happy with the quality of information provided to them.

The elders threatened to sue the company for the theft of their intellectual property - she had been employed by them as their pastor so consequentially any work undertaken during said period of her engagement belonged to them, not to her. They had on record the permission they granted her to embark on the project on their behalf - she had no right to receive any remuneration for this consultancy - all monies paid to her should be reimbursed to the church together with a sum for damages.

Unfortunately, the particulars provided by the church was in direct contradiction to the contract she had signed with the company.

It then all got a little bit messy and there were some extremely unpleasant arguments with her new husband who felt she was responsible for the mess he found himself at the epicentre of. The imbroglio was finally resolved by the company secretary and head of legal services - she would repay all the monies she had received erroneously and the Church of Universal Values would be paid a suitably adequate lump sum for the work together with an amount for any undue inconvenience caused by the unfortunate affair.

In reality both her and the church where proverbially screwed by the deal - no-one at the time realised just how financially profitable the SPPA™, as developed from her thesis, would actually be.

She sued for divorce from her husband 21 months later. He didn't like her drinking and use of recreational drugs and she, quite simply, didn't like him - she never had, it was a convenient relationship to escape from the hole she had inadvertently dug for herself - it had been an act of self-preservation on her part. She endured the mandatory sex for a while and then 'Big Daddy' took pity on her and inflicted a prostate problem on the old git, the treatment of which rendered him impotent.

In the absence of sex he began to resent her even more, and she divorced him on the grounds of unreasonable behaviour.

It transpired his unreasonable behaviour could be boiled down to not approving or allowing her to go out to all night parties, clubs, festivals, and failing to provide her with the sufficient resources to fund her need for alcohol and recreational drugs. She had been hoping for a generous financial settlement. Whilst her ex-husband was indeed required to provide her with a little alimony, it was considered she had not contributed anything of significant value to the 21 months of their marital bliss which would justify anything more substantial.

Well, she has now spent almost all the money she was awarded, along with the paltry inheritance she received from her mother six months ago. Being one of seven siblings she was never likely to have received much from her mother, and, as her father had done previously, the mother inserted a clause into her will to deduct from the evangelist's share a number of outstanding loans made to her in the past.

Her brothers and sisters no longer engage with her being more than aware of her financial need and proclivity to spend whatever she can scavenge on drugs and alcohol. Yet again she is currently homeless and has nowhere to sleep tonight. What little cash she has on her person will be required to pay for a room in a hostel.

She is feeling her age, in fact she feels older than her years, she is nearing fifty. Well, she never thought she would make it this far anyway. She is dressed in her favourite clothes - a multi coloured long length skirt with a fashionable jacket covering a plain pink clerical shirt with dog collar. On her feet is a pair of salmon-coloured boots. Around her neck and falling onto her chest is a pendant - It is a cross crafted in ebony wood resting on a golden six-pointed star partially enclosed in a double silver circle - a facsimile of the cross hanging over the altar - the very same symbol she had been researching in the church archives.

Whilst you may have thought she would want to hide her profession, she doesn't. The clerical outfit gives her an air of respectability and whilst she does not have a recognisable license to preach, the fact she is a reverend reveals she has at least completed a four year ministerial course in a reputable theological college and she is therefore a person who can be trusted.

Nonetheless, the clothes, rather like herself, appear slightly tired and worn. Her hair is no longer the magnificently brilliant red of the past - it is naturally greying. However, she continues to maintain the previous colour through the regular application of an off the shelf colouring kit. What was once luxurious and soft is now looking a trifle thin and dry. Whilst many would still describe her as youthful and attractive, if you look closely, behind the make-up you will see the fine lines of an older age peeking through on a papery thin skin.

She has finally had to conclude there is a finite limit to the number of sofas she can continue to sleep on. She appears to have outgrown the charity of friends she could once rely on.

She can't remember what exactly happened the previous night but she obviously got drunk. Her one and only remaining and relatively friendly acquaintance was deeply unimpressed by her behaviour, informing her this morning she was no longer welcome and should remove herself from the sofa as quickly as possible.

She is now homeless once again with nowhere obvious to go (other than the hostel), hence she is sitting in this coffee shop contemplating her future. There will no longer be any redemptive welcome from her regular circuit of forgiving churches - she has a reputation, one which appears to be countrywide - she is not to be trusted. Of course, everyone simply misunderstands her needs and do not value the blessings of god she could bestow on them in return for their assistance.

No, she has not enjoyed her life recently. She feels a sense of lack, a hole in her soul which 'Big Daddy' no longer seems willing to fill. She had always perceived of herself as being young. Then after the divorce and the death of her mother she had the dawning cognisance this was no longer the case - that she had in fact well and truly arrived into her middle age.

She sets down the large cup of coffee back onto the table and places her hands on her knees and follows her breathing. For a couple of seconds she realises the totality of her being, then instantly loses it as she comprehends the actuality of her current predicament. The sensation leaves her body as her emotion captures the endeavour and numbs the pain of her reality - to daydream feels good.

Her current situation is relatively simple to encapsulate. Since her divorce the drugs and alcohol no longer provide any sustenance toward the maintenance of her relationship with the world. The latest generation of society does not appreciate her - they have their own unique ideas, beliefs and culture which she simply does not understand - she is too old for them -

she doesn't empathise with them, there is no connection and she is unable to communicate with them on any level - they are too young.

As for her own generation, her special congregation, they have either died, got married, had children, found jobs and developed their own careers, or simply disowned her. She has no role to play - her career as an itinerant minister of religion is over. She has played all the cards, and there are none left in the pack - she is no longer the welcomed prodigal child - she is now too old to play the game. Even 'Big Daddy' has stopped talking to her - she is abandoned, lonely and most definitely fed up.

She places her hands on her knees and decides it's time to try and fix the line to 'Big Daddy'. She closes her eyes and begins to silently pray - begging for an end to her suffering - imploring him to send a message to show he had not forsaken her - pleading with him to provide sustenance in her life. For a moment she becomes the prayer - all her attention is focussed on her god. Then as quickly as she finds it she loses the focus of her attention as she identifies yet again with the actuality of her current dilemma.

The morose chain of thoughts she experiences is suddenly broken on noticing an old man walk into the coffee shop. He is wearing an aged threadbare black cassock, which although clean has obviously seen better days. He stands at the door and looks around the room appearing to seek someone out. Their eyes meet and he stares at her for a moment before walking over to the counter to order and pay for a cup of earl grey tea. He looks at her again - he seems strangely familiar but she can't remember having ever met the old man before - surely she would remember.

The old man in the cassock walks down the coffee house with his cup of tea towards her table and sits down in front of her without being invited.

"Do you know who I am, perchance?" He enquires.

The evangelist looks at him. "A man of the cloth, I presume. Most probably of the catholic variety if you choose to wear a black cassock in town - especially one that appears to be a tad threadbare."

The old man in the threadbare cassock looks puzzled for a moment and seems to be searching for something to say. When he finally speaks the evangelist senses the subtle harmonics of an acerbic bitterness in the tonal quality of his voice.

"I am not a catholic priest. I am your predecessor - I was the pastor of the Church of Universal Values until they retired me to make way for you! I have some questions I need answered - I seek to understand your reasoning for dissembling the truth of our mutual heritage."

The evangelist is suddenly startled. She had seen him before, they kept a photographic record of all the previous incumbent pastors on the wall of the vestry, he was her predecessor. What the hell did he want with her?

"As I recall you had already been retired before I was interviewed for the post. In case you don't know my appointment didn't go very well and I was, in absence of a better expression, sacked. They didn't want and couldn't listen to the truth I gave them."

The old man in the threadbare cassock responds immediately.

"And as I understand the situation you were removed from your post because you were a drug ridden alcoholic who had stolen, in absence of a better expression, their family silver together with a substantial amount of money." There was a degree of intensity laced within the sound of his voice as he said this, yet as he spoke he was actually smiling at her as if the response was merely a game to attain her attention. It succeeded, he had.

"How did you know I was here?" The evangelist asks.

"I asked god and I was told you would be here."

"Lucky you. god seems to have stopped talking to me."

"God never stops talking - people just lose their ability to listen. A lack of intention and attention is generally the cause. And it is your intention I am seeking to understand. Our meeting is advantageous, I promise you. I am giving you a chance to redeem yourself and pay off your karmic debt."

He looks across and sees the pendant hanging around her neck. She notices his glance and immediately moves her left hand up to her throat to caress it.

"It was given to me by the elders of the church when I was inducted as their minister. I treasure it very much."

"Obviously you didn't treasure it that much or you would not have created the ludicrous fiction surrounding its meaning and sold it on to RLE Incorporated Limited to be turned into their preposterous psychometric assessment?"

The evangelist pauses for a moment and removes her hand from the pendant. "As you are more than aware all the Pastors prior to me were mentored and inducted into their post by their predecessor. I wasn't and therefore I was completely unaware of the Church of Universal Values' 'legacy' which I was being required to administer. So, to make up for my lack I sat with all the old ledgers held within the archives and read the ramblings of the original pastor and his son. It just so happened to coincide with the time the company approached the church to discover more about the origins of an image they were using as their company logo, an image which just happens to be identical to the pendant hanging around my neck.

"I had never ever before had the privilege of reading so much garbage and half-baked esoteric nonsense in the whole of my life. Nevertheless, with prayer and the guidance of god, I finally managed to make some sort of sense from it and finally understood god's hidden purpose contained within the symbol. It was this I submitted on behalf of the church to RLE Incorporated Limited. I was never paid for my research, regardless of what you may have become to believe. We are both servants of our lord and I was doing only what I was inspired by him to do. This was my truth as revealed by him in that particular moment in time. It is god's purpose I was fulfilling and as our lord said, 'and you will know the truth and the truth will set you free.'"

The old man in the threadbare cassock smiles. "John chapter 8, verse 32. And in verse 34 he goes on to say, 'Truly, truly I say unto you, everyone who practices sin is a slave to sin.' Tell me, how do you know you did not miss the mark in this matter?"

"The closer you are to god the less likely you are to miss the mark. The further away from god and yes, you would be more likely to miss the mark. 'For if we go on sinning deliberately after receiving the knowledge of truth, there no longer remains a sacrifice for sins' Hebrews chapter 10, verse 26."

"And yet you have just told me god is no longer speaking to you. Now I would suggest this reveals you are very definitely missing the mark."

"Quite simply, I was very close to god at the time - he spoke to me frequently. Whatever is happening to me now is my responsibility to resolve, it has to do with this moment, nothing to do with the past."

"And yet the best predictor of future behaviour is the behaviour of the past." mutters the old man in the threadbare cassock.

The evangelist parries the comment immediately "Søren Kierkegaard once said, 'life can only be understood looking backwards but must be lived forwards.' I would argue he was wrong - it has to be lived in the moment. Truth lies in the moment, which is where I happened to be at the time I wrote the treatise - close to god."

"Yet what you wrote and how it was interpreted was not based on the prevailing historical and esoteric information you held within your hands at the time. As you have already pointed out you did not have me as your mentor when you entered that church, if you had I would have explained it all to you."

"And your explanation would have been biased, as indeed your response to me in this moment is. Your truth is merely your own personal perspective and where you exist in relation to the line of your being. You are an older man, and there is probably a degree of unconscious bias in how you perceive reality."

"I believe in the reality of truth - your truth is falsehood." He growls.

'However, your truth may not be reality either - where is the line between either truth or falsehood? Now personally I have had enough of this conversation and would like to be left alone to finish my coffee in peace. I have more than enough to worry about without discussing something which occurred in the past over which neither you nor I have any control. It is in the hand of god."

There is a silence in the moment. The old man in the threadbare cassock looks at the evangelist pensively, perhaps even a little whimsically. When he finally speaks he does so thoughtfully with the subtlest hint of gentleness.

"You are not what I was expecting. You really are actually quite an intelligent woman - in many respects it would have been interesting to be your mentor, though I doubt if anything I could have given you would have profited your life in any way. You are right - it is in the hand of god." He stands up and leaves.

The evangelist sighs and returns to the solitary contemplation of her coffee cup.

A few minutes later she hears the sound of someone yet again sitting down in the seat opposite to her without her invitation. The old man in the threadbare cassock has obviously returned to impart some further critique on her life. She doesn't even bother to look up.

"I thought I asked you to leave, please go. I have nothing further to say.

She hears a slight giggle, it is musical and sweet. "But I have only just got here, surely you don't want me to go just yet. I wanted to talk to you. You are a servant of the lord judging by your apparel. Surely you're not off duty." There is a delicate laugh which floats upon the air towards the evangelist.

The evangelist looks up and sees a young women sat in front of her. She is tall, with a delicate yet strong face, she is dressed in a long white summer dress with a silver link chain holding a bright green emerald pendant. Her eyes seem to give off a golden sheen making it impossible to ascertain their actual colouring. Her hair is of the most glorious light auburn and hangs down to her waist - she is beautiful and obviously very rich.

"Well it looks like it's my lucky day - though I have certainly not been short of conversation so far. How can I help you?"

The young lady with the light auburn hair looks at her and smiles. "Oh I don't know, I just came in and saw you there and you looked so sad. I thought a conversation might cheer you up. You look lonely, are you? I will go if you want me to."

The evangelist is enthralled by the beauty, the sweetness of the remark, and, of course, the apparent wealth of the person sat opposite her. She contemplates the situation and realises she will need to play this particular game carefully. She might just find somewhere to stay for the next few days.

"What would you like to talk about?" The evangelist asks.

The young lady with the light auburn hair smiles revealing what the evangelist considers to be the most perfect set of pearly white teeth she has ever seen. She feels a strong attraction to this woman.

The young lady with the light auburn hair responds. "Why don't you ask me a question. A question is always a good way to start a conversation."

The evangelist considers this for a moment. She needs to find out more about this woman, and the potential for a relationship with her.

"Have you ever been married."

"No, in my particular world it has never been relevant. Marriage is a human construct and a fabricated institution - I guess it helps some people feel secure in your world. I have no need for such a particular security. What about you?"

"Once," laughed the evangelist, "and it proved to be a very insecure experience. I am now divorced. Men or women, who are you attracted to?"

The young lady with the auburn smiles another radiant smile. "If you are referring to sexual attraction I have to say I am of a generation and age where such things hold no importance. I love everyone for who they are. What about you?"

"Both boys and girls when I was interested and had the urge. I don't get that particular itch so often now." The evangelist grimaces. "I am not sure I have ever had a serious relationship, they generally only last around seven months. I have never achieved the full octave. Even though I stayed with my husband for 21 months - it never really counted - we were not suitable for each other right from the beginning - it was a question of compatibility and he failed to provide the correct answer. My only true relationship was with god but he doesn't seem to be speaking to me anymore."

The young lady with the light auburn hair looks serious for a moment. "You know god never stops talking. Maybe you have just temporarily lost the sensitivity to hear. It does happen."

The evangelist is startled. "Someone else just told me something very similar a few moments ago. Are you in cahoots with him? If you are I really don't need another lecture about my life today. What do you want?"

The evangelist notices the young lady with the light auburn hair is smiling and looking at her, could it be possible, with an expression of unconditional love? She feels it radiate from the lady surrounding her in a mantel of unquestioning compassion, which in turn generates an unmistakeable sensation of peace within her.

"What do you want?" The young lady with the auburn hair replies.

"I want the peace I am feeling right now never to leave me."

"Have you never known peace before?"

The young lady with the light auburn hair holds the evangelist eyes within her own. The evangelist is transfixed - the eyes seem even more radiant than before. In a moment lasting for an eternity the evangelist feels compelled to look back over the totality of her life - every action, every deed, seems to pass in front of her eyes. She wants to answer the question truthfully.

"I think I was I was only ever truly happy when I was talking to god, but I don't really know now."

The young lady with the light auburn hair looks at the evangelist - the colour of her eyes appear to be golden.

"God is always here, God is with us now and maybe you just need to move a little closer to your heart's desire." She pauses and for a moment the evangelist looks directly into her golden eyes. "Look the sun is shining."

The evangelist looks towards the door and the sun is indeed shining brightly through it. The lady with the light auburn hair continues.

 "Would you like to come home with me. I know you need somewhere to stay and you will be very welcome in my house."

She stands up from her chair and extends her left hand out toward the evangelist. The evangelist suddenly feels a lightness of being as if all the troubles of her world have suddenly left her. She smiles at the young lady with the light auburn hair, raises herself from her seat, and takes hold of her hand. They walk to the sunlit door oblivious of all the other customers in the coffee shop. As they approach the door the young lady with the auburn hair turns to the evangelist.

"Don't worry about internet access, there is more connectivity in my house than you will ever have experienced before."

****

Thirty minutes later the barista walks over to the evangelist's table to see if she is ok. She has been noticed sat slumped with her face resting on her left cheek on the table apparently staring at her large cup of coffee.

Her eyes are wide open – unblinking - it is obvious she is unwell - in fact, much to the alarm of everyone in the coffee shop, she is dead.

Following a post mortem the coroner concluded the evangelist had suffered a sudden arrhythmic cardiac arrest caused by long term drug and alcohol abuse.

Chapter 9 - The Guru

> 'Very few will contemplate the reality of their death
> Whilst dreaming within the confines of their sleep.'

"Where are my apricots?" The Guru bangs his left hand on the table in frustration, looks around and thumps the table again. "Where is the milk - why isn't there any milk? Why call me for breakfast before the table has been set properly? We eat the same breakfast every day surely it cannot be beyond your capability to set it up properly, especially when we have an important visitor staying with us."

An elderly supplicant rushes into the dining refectory room from the kitchen clutching a bowl of apricots and places it in front of the Guru.

The Guru looks at the fruit closely and glares at the supplicant.

"This is not good enough. These apricots are not ripe - I will not eat unripe fruit." He picks up one piece of fruit and waves it under the nose of the supplicant. "Where did they come from? Surely at this time of year there are ripe apricots to be found in the markets?"

The supplicant looks down in shame with his eyes towards his feet.

"They come from the metro supermarket in town, Guruji. We have not had the time to go to the farmers market - there are too few of us remaining, and then there are all the other chores you require of us."

"Take them away and stew them with a little syrup – then I will eat them with my daliya."

The Guru sighs and descends into an oppressive silence that fills the room and surrounds everyone present with an impenetrable fog of negativity. There is no question - the negativity is being transmitted by the Guru - is this his intention?

It is a large dining hall and once upon a time the kitchen would serve up to two hundred covers per meal for the resident supplicants and the regular visitors. Today there are only twenty-three people sat around the main table at the head of the room. All the other trestles remain empty and devoid of any apparel which would indicate they have been used anytime recently or are likely to be utilised again in the near future.

Another supplicant brings in a jug of hot milk. The Guru looks up as she places the jug in his hands. He sighs and in a dispassionate voice instructs her to return it to the kitchen.

"It is not hot enough - the jug needs to be rinsed with boiling water before placing the milk in it, in future please remember to do so - you have been told this many times before."

The Guru sighs deeply again and yawns, opening his mouth wide to reveal a full set of gleaming white teeth. The oppressive silence returns once more. The residents of the table sit quietly not risking to look at one another, let alone the Guru, awaiting an intimation from him breakfast can commence and the bowls of daliya placed in front of them may be consumed.

The Guru looks up and down the table appearing to be searching for something. He sighs deeply again. "Where is my special bread? Fetch me my bread and make sure it is toasted properly."

No-one questions the motives behind the Guru's regular outbursts or the overwhelming negativity he chooses to emanate upon them on a daily basis, for he is very old and venerable.

Very few remember a time when he was not the central teaching figure of the Ashram. All the supplicants at the table have been at the Ashram for many years and might be perceived as being somewhat elderly themselves. Yet none of them would remotely dare to contemplate that their Guru may not be the enlightened teacher possessing the answers to their long-held questions regarding the nature of their being.

The Visitor sits quietly observing the faces of the Guru's disciples whilst registering the stifling negativity surrounding him. He is a seeker of truth yet whatever truth there is at this moment it appears to contain very little love - if any such energy had ever existed in this place it appears to have been squashed back within the kernel of its seed. He suddenly feels the impact of someone staring at him - it is the Guru looking directly at him.

"So you came here seeking the truth - would you really like to know the truth?" The Guru looks inquisitively at the Visitor and then glares at his disciples and snarls. "Well it remains hidden behind the lies of the disciples.

"Every truth ever revealed has been cloaked within the fundamentalist views surrounding its discovery. Very slowly the roots of its creation are sucked back down into the fertile ground from whence they sprang and the plant slowly withers - and yet the memorial of its discovery remains firmly in the memories of the devotees - the memorial itself is not the truth and yet this is all they will worship.

"A wise man once said, 'always tell the truth', alas he died a fool. A wiser man said, 'never tell a lie for in that way the truth is revealed'. He died a saviour to many - alas the truth of his life also became a lie.

"Normally within less than thirty years following the death of a true teacher the followers will fall off the cliff of understanding. Occasionally the truth behind the facade will be found by a devout seeker. Unfortunately for the many, those who believe only at the level of magic – they will die disappointed."

He smiles at the Visitor before continuing. "Of course all truth has its source within the vine of its creation and yet it is not of the tree of life. It is separated by a subtle line, barely visible to the ordinary eye. And yet it appears that every day you, personally, experience the dividing mark between truth and the lie - the line which is so thin most ordinary people end up experiencing falsehood and truth together as if it were one and the same - you feel and see it, maybe even taste it. Is this not your true nature?"

The Visitor looks at the Guru carefully before considering his answer. "In many respects all I know are the lies. Whilst I feel the truth in what others say, I only know what they are saying is true to them. When I draw as part of my daily meditation a truth is revealed, but I rarely if ever see the truth of what I portray until after the event has occurred."

The Guru considers the Visitor for a moment, "well maybe you should just carry-on drawing and open up the art gallery of your dreams."

He stares morosely at his portion of daliya in front of him before suddenly deciding to continue his conversation. "Unless of course you are so egotistical to believe you create the truth through your own drawing, or through the dissemination of false interpretations of the truth through your business.

"We all have the power to create but we are blissfully unaware of the impact of our creations, as I believe you are slowly coming to realise." He looks up toward the visitor giving him a knowing and sly smile.

Seeing there will be no reply forthcoming from the Visitor he continues waiting for his stewed apricots and his hot milk.

Suddenly he strikes the table with both his fists and shouts loudly. "Where is my toast?!"

The female supplicant rushes back into the room clutching the jug of hot milk and a plate of toast. She places them both in front of him.

"Why is there so much toast? I can't eat all of this. It is a waste." He sighs again. He remains sitting still.

The Visitor looks across the table at the Guru who appears to be sourly contemplating his breakfast and suddenly feels a sense of amusement over the drama playing out in front of him. In the ensuing silence he finds himself considering what his own role is in this piece of theatre and his unique personal responsibility as the guest at the table.

Clearly this little performance is being played out for his benefit. Although he is not a pupil he realises he must pay an appropriate respect to the elderly gentleman sitting opposite who is the revered teacher to all these other people.

Is he himself being tested? And if so for what purpose? He decides to ask a question.

His motive is simplistic in origin although his unconscious bias is one of superiority to everyone else sat at the table held in thrall to this old man - he wants to try and break the silence and the spell the Guru is obviously holding over all of them. He asks the question - there is an intention and yet it commences with an unintentional cough.

"I was just thinking - how did and Englishman end up becoming the Guru of an Ashram in Northern India?"

Within the brooding silence there is a palpable gasp - how dare the Visitor break the unspoken rule of silence. It is the Guru and the Guru only who indicates when a question may be asked - only he grants the permission to break silence.

The old man continues to sit silently contemplating his breakfast.

After what seems to be an interminable interval, during which everyone, including the visitor, begins to assume the Guru has failed to hear what the Visitor has asked, he replies without moving a muscle.

"You are thinking too much. Maybe you should return to your feeling. Your question is inadequate for what you are trying to achieve - one might even go as far to suggest you are being coercive in an environment where you are the welcome guest. You are already aware of my story - you were told it prior to your arrival. So, would you like to ask me a question relating to what you were truthfully trying to achieve? After all it is the truth you are seeking here, as you so carefully explained in your letter requesting an audience with me. I assume you were telling the truth?"

The Visitor's sense of superiority vanishes in an instant. He is aware he has reacted inappropriately in asking the question - he feels remorse. He makes an apology. The Guru looks up at him and smiles in acknowledgement.

The negativity evaporates instantly and the Visitor cannot help but notice the slightest hint of a smile appearing on all the faces of all those sat at the table. Assuming they might start their breakfast they pick up their spoons.

"No you may not eat yet. There is a question to be answered and whilst everyone is welcome at this table we must not let our standards drop. You know what is required from each and every one of you, and the lack of numbers in our ranks does not change the nature of our search."

An oppressive atmosphere returns instantly - although this time it is lighter in appearance and flavour. The Guru has been engaged - everyone feels relieved.

"I will accept your apology for what was an ill-considered, incorrectly conceived and poorly formulated question. It was not the question that should have been asked, nevertheless, I am obliged to answer it as postulated.

"My father's father came here many years ago. He was sent on a sabbatical mission to explore the foundation of christian culture and arrived here enquiring about a symbol resembling a Celtic cross situated within our adjacent temple.

"He stayed here for ten years. My father's mother was acquainted with my grandfather during his ministry in a church in an affluent parish near the city where you live and she came out to visit the Ashram. It was during the festival of Holi when my father was conceived.

"My grandfather left the Ashram upon hearing of the death of my grandmother, returning to take care of the son he had been blissfully unaware of.

"He returned an egoist with the arrogance required to found a church based on the most minimal understanding of the truths he had supposedly discovered whilst he was here.

"My father, being relieved to find a male parent he could look up to, succumbed to his inherent narcissism and followed him in his misguided ministry. I refused to follow either of them, although it was supposedly my destiny to become the minister of the Church of Universal Values, and instead I sought the source of truth which is hidden here in full view within the Ashram and the temple."

He pauses and looks at the visitor closely before continuing.

"If you choose to stay with me for a while I will lead you on the path towards truth. Consider my offer carefully for you do have ability and you are most welcome here."

The elderly supplicant enters the room just as the Guru finishes speaking, clutching a bowl of apricots gently stewed with a little syrup. The Guru smiles and the breakfast is allowed to commence.

"Breakfast is one of the main changes I brought about when I took over from my own Guruji. My digestive system is somewhat sensitive - it has been for many years following a bout of dysentery I developed shortly after arriving here. Porridge or muesli soaked overnight with the correct rehydrated fruit and spices, together with some fresh fruit is all one really needs before work begins. Nevertheless, they still need their little breads and pickles to keep them happy. So I have a special bread - it is made for me every day. Would you care to try a slice?"

A silent gasp emerges once more. No-one is allowed to taste the Guru's special bread. The Guru notices and growls at the supplicants.

"He is English, I am English, you are not. He will appreciate my bread in a way you never could, in the same way I will never appreciate your pickles. Now let us break our fast in peace. We have a lot of work to do in the garden today." He turns to look at the Visitor, "You will join me there, of course…"

The Visitor had arrived the night before. He was supposed to have been met at the rail station at the local town but there was no-one there to meet him.

He waited for fifteen minutes before calling the Ashram on the telephone number he had been given in case he was delayed in any way. There was no answer.

Finally he decided to hire a taxi to take him and his luggage to the Ashram. He managed to flag down an auto rickshaw just outside the station. He asked the driver to take him to the Ashram. The man had looked at him in surprise.

"Sahib, why go there? No-one ever goes there now. The old man is crazy - he is no guru. I know a good hotel run by my cousin. Let me take you there?"

The Visitor explained he was going to the Ashram at the request of the Aunt - he was to scatter her ashes in the holy Ganges near the temple just outside the Ashram.

"Aha, I understand now, you do it for Aunty. I will take you there at once."

The driver picked up the luggage, placed it in the back of the rickshaw and the Visitor stepped in and made himself comfortable. They drove through the town and thirteen minutes later arrived at the gates of the Ashram. The Visitor got out of the back of the rickshaw and walked over to the gates. The driver jumped out and followed him.

The gates were partially open, not in any intentional way but as if someone had carelessly forgotten to close them properly. The Visitor looked through the gates down the long avenue toward the temple. The layout was exactly as he expected it to be based on the photographs he had seen of the Ashram whilst planning his journey. There were the four long buildings facing each other - the administration buildings, meeting hall and refectory on the left and the residential accommodation for guest and longer-term residents on the right.

However, his living memory of the photographs were more alive to him than what he was experiencing in the moment. The whole place seemed derelict. There was no discernible lighting and the garden itself looked as if it had been left to go to wrack and ruin. The driver surveyed the look on his passenger's face with concern.

"It is as I said, Sahib, no-one comes here anymore. Are they expecting you? Let me take you to my cousin's hotel. It is not far away and you can come back tomorrow."

The Visitor began to doubt himself. Had he come on the wrong day? Was this the actual Ashram he had arranged to visit? He took out the letter with all the instructions he had been given. It was all there, the date to arrive, the train to take, the fact he would be met at the station, and the telephone number he should ring if there was any problem. He showed it to the driver who examined it carefully.

"I will walk you down with your luggage to the administration office. It is in the first building on the left. Let us see if anyone is there."

Within the deepening evening darkness they walked slowly down the avenue footpaths toward the building. As they approached the main door the visitor could make out a dim light, possibly from candles, glowing warmly through the ground floor windows. He felt a small sigh of relief easing through his body. He now noticed the tension which had slowly built up through his body from the moment he had arrived at the rail station. He became aware of his breathing, relaxed immediately and laughed silently to himself.

How had he allowed himself to become so anxious by the situation he had found himself in? He paused for a moment and smiled - everything was OK - good in fact.

The reality was he was way outside his habitual comfort zone - he had been ever since he arrived into the Indian sub-continent - it was, in the circumstances, hardly surprising he would occasionally feel apprehensive.

They arrived at the door and the visitor turned the handle to check it was not locked. He turned to the driver, thanked him for his assistance, and handed him a five hundred rupee note insisting the driver should keep the change. The driver looked confused.

"Sahib, this is a lot of money for the journey from the rail station. Are you sure?"

The Visitor assured him he was.

"Namaste. In this case I will go back to the gate and wait for a while. If they do not make you welcome I will take you to my cousin's hotel at no extra cost."

He turned, placed his hands together and bowed toward the visitor before making his way slowly back up the path toward the gate, turning around occasionally to check on his passenger. The Visitor watched him for a few moments before moving his attention toward the door. After a momentary pause he turned the handle and walked into a small reception room and stood in the doorway.

Opposite the door was an ornate wooden reception desk of the colonial age on which sat a brass handbell, its wooden handle carved with a motif of the God Hanuman. Stretching halfway down the left-hand side wall was a large shoe cabinet crafted in sheesham wood housing nineteen pairs of shoes, and at the lower end of the wall several lines of coat hooks, currently unoccupied. There was a double door in the centre of the right-hand side wall. On each side of the door were two portraits of ancient venerable men dressed in orange robes with white straggly beards and long hair sitting in various meditative postures. The Visitor guessed, correctly in fact, that these were portraits of previous Swamis of the Ashram.

The Visitor entered the reception and could immediately discern the low murmur of an individual's voice, talking as if in conversation. He was not sure what to do, what the etiquette of the situation required of him. Surely it would not be polite to walk in through the door unannounced. He decides to ring the reception bell and wait.

He picks up the bell in his left hand. He finds the balance rather reassuring. Slowly he swings the bell from left to right to left before returning it to the centre. Two deeply resonant and harmonically pleasing chimes ring out. It is much louder than he expected and he has no doubt it must have been audible in the room beyond the doors. He awaits for a response. There is none.

After a few minutes he walks slowly to the double doors and pauses for a moment and slowly places his hand on the right doorknob, twists it, and slowly opens the door. The hinges let out a slow monotonous moan as if awaking from a long stupor and not expecting to have to undertake any strenuous work.

He stands at the entrance of what transpires to be a dining refectory with the walls painted in an old dingy off-white brown paint interspersed with various pictures of the Vedic pantheon of deities.

All the tables are empty bar the one stretched lengthways along the wall at the far end of the room opposite the doorway. Around the table are sat twenty-two people, who immediately fall silent and turn to look at him. There was a door behind the table and two alcoves like windows.

At first glance the visitor is reminded of Leonardo de Vinci's mural painting of the last supper. However, in the centre of the table, raised slightly higher than the companions, is not Jesus, but an old Caucasian man with a long grey beard and equally lengthy straggling white hair. He stares imperiously at the visitor as the whole room becomes energised in anticipation.

"Where have you been?! I have been awaiting you for some time now. You have arrived during our Satsang - never mind. Come closer let me see what you are."

The Guru, for this is the man addressing him, speaks with an impeccable southern English accent. For a moment the Visitor is confused, this was not what he was expecting. Slowly he gains composure - surely the old man must know he was supposed to be met at the station.

"I am sorry - I got here as quickly as I could, but I was expecting to be met at the rail station in accordance with the instructions given in the letter sent by the Ashram's secretary."

"Nevertheless," growled the Guru, "I was expecting you to arrive long before today." Suddenly the Guru turns to glare at the man sat next to him. "Why was no-one there to meet him at the rail station. This is a clear dereliction of your duties as Ashram secretary. Is it time to replace you with another useless administrator?"

The secretary smiled - he seemed oblivious to the old man's outburst, as if he was expecting some sort of retort to the one which had just been delivered. "But Guruji, you told us not to go and fetch him. You said he was to find his own way here."

The Guru ignores the remark and turns his glare away to scrutinise the Visitor more closely.

The Visitor felt a small degree of amusement at the interaction. He could taste the truth behind the peculiar discourse. It was all true how could that be? His mind wandered only for a moment before he was startled back into the room by the voice of the Guru addressing him.

"So you are tasting the truth and find it confusing, hardly surprising for one so young on the path? Anyway, you are here now and you have finally managed to walk through a door. Have you brought her with you?"

The Visitor was once again confused - what was the old man talking about? He remains silent not knowing what to say.

"The ashes, you fool." Snarled the Guru. "Did you bring her ashes like she requested? Surely you are not as dumb as these senseless idiots." He waved his hand in a circular movement indicating he was referring to everyone sat around the table with him. They all dropped their heads towards the floor sheepishly.

Suddenly it all made sense. The old man must be the friend the Aunt had spoken of in her letter.

"Yes, I have brought them with me. As I explained in my letter to the Ashram she asked if the monks would perform the appropriate ritual for the scattering of her ashes into the Ganges."

"Maybe we will. Maybe I won't. Let us wait and see when it would be auspicious to undertake the water ceremony. In the meantime bring her into me."

The visitor turned away from the table and returned to the reception where he had left his luggage. He opened a rucksack and removed a circular wooden urn crafted in beech wood.

Holding it in both hands he walks slowly and carefully back into the room, conscious of every footstep he places on the floor. He walks over to the table and hands it over to the Guru.

The Guru takes the urn, sets it down on the table in front of him, and places both hands around it. He murmurs what appears to be a prayer. He looks up at the table of eager faces waiting eagerly to hear him speak.

"We promised one day we would meet again and remain within each other's company forever. I am not sure this is what we meant." He speaks quietly at first as if talking to himself. Then his voice rises in volume addressing all present. "We were lovers many years ago and explored the eroticism of Kamadeva together. We were very young in the ways of the world. She left here after a few months and returned to the city of our birth - I remained here to be a blessing to you all. Satsang is now over."

The Guru turns to the secretary. "Take our visitor to the guest house and make sure he is given a pleasing room with a view over the gardens."

Turning to the Visitor he continues. "The morning bell rings at 5am, we meet in the main hall for prayer and yoga at 6am. Breakfast will be at 8.30am. I expect you to join us at 6am. I am now returning to my rooms." With that he stands up and leaves the refectory through the door behind the table without any further glance towards the people sat around the table or the Visitor.

For a moment all was so silent it seemed everyone, including the Visitor, had stopped breathing. Suddenly there was the gasp of expiration followed by the babel of voices as everyone found their ability to speak once more.

The secretary turned to the Visitor, "they will calm down shortly. The idea of the Guru practising the Kama Sutra is beyond their reasoning. I myself would doubt he has ever been intimate with anyone - certainly not since I came here and that was many years ago. Celibacy is the generally condoned condition for residents of the ashram though not a conditional demand.

"Celibacy arises naturally within everyone who stays here for a while - they discover there is no longer a need or urge to gratify the flesh in a carnal way. This is why my companions are currently experiencing a state of consternation.

"I would assume the Guruji was intentionally trying to shock them in his never-ending quest to keep them awake and prevent them from falling asleep. Come, let me take you to the guest room we have prepared for you."

The Visitor followed the secretary out of the refectory into the reception room where he was surprised to find his luggage was no longer where he had left it. He turned to the secretary with an inquiring look. The secretary smiled. "I have already arranged for all your luggage to be taken to your room."

They walked into the garden and the secretary took out a torch and shone it over the path weaving its way through the flower and vegetable beds across towards the accommodation blocks. The moon and stars were shining brightly in the night-time sky. The secretary turned to the visitor:

"We are near the time of the full moon and this provides us long-term residents with more than enough light to find our way through the garden pathways - we walk them time and time again knowing the line each path takes. This is your first time on this path so I will endeavour to illuminate your way."

Having arrived at the accommodation block, the secretary led him through an open archway door. They then walked up fourteen steps to what was to be his bedroom. The secretary opened the door, stood back and allowed the Visitor to enter. It was a small simple room with a single bed, a wardrobe, and a washstand with a jug of water next to it. The large double window at the end of the room opened out onto a small wooden balcony.

"This is the room we traditionally house our most important European male visitors. The Guruji himself resided in this room when he first came here. I will leave you to settle in and rest. We will meet again in the morning for the meditation and yoga session. This will be held in the main hall which is in the other block next to the administration building and refectory."

The secretary placed his hands together and bowed giving a personal Namaste before walking back down the stairs and into the garden.

The Visitor laid down on the bed and considered the ceiling for a moment before he fell, fully clothed, into a deep sleep.

Following the morning prayer, yoga and breakfast he returned to his room and started to unpack his suitcase, hanging his shirts, trousers and jackets on the coat hangers in the wardrobe, and placing his socks, pants and tee-shirts in the small drawers placed for this purpose at the foot of the wardrobe.

After selecting a shirt and a pair of trousers he considered suitable for working in the garden he took off the clothes he had been wearing for breakfast, folded them and laid them carefully at the end of the bed. Once he had changed into his work clothes he walked out onto the veranda and looked down onto the garden.

He could see the grounds had been laid out thoughtfully into carefully considered sections. Though even in the daylight it was abundantly clear the garden had seen better days. Much of planting had been allowed to grow beyond the space comfortable for them. The rows of vegetables were infested with weeds. There had been some attempts to tame the wild excesses of the plants, however the pruning appeared to have been undertaken in crude, confrontational and aggressive manner. Then he saw the old man walking towards the vegetable patch with two hoes on a wheelbarrow.

The old man looked up to the veranda and beckoned the Visitor to join him.

He returned to his bedroom, walked down the fourteen steps, through the open archway door and into the garden.

The old man looked at him and smiled. "Thank you for accompanying me in my morning travails. There is too much to do on my own and I am no longer as agile as I once was - I become fatigued far too easily these days."

"Where is everyone else?" Inquired the Visitor, "surely the others in the community should be out here to help you."

The old man laughed derisively. "They are busy in the office earning the money we require in order to continue our existence here."

The Visitor looked at him inquisitively.

"They are busy responding to my online community of followers and letter writers. I have a reputation, not necessarily unfounded, of being a wise man capable of giving forthright advise and meditations to guide people on their spiritual quest.

"I receive a great deal of correspondence both online and through the postal system, generally accompanied, I have to admit, with significant financial contributions to our coffers from people who are too lazy to Work for themselves. They seek an easy way towards enlightenment and I happily provide them with an easing balm, giving them words of comfort to ease the nightmares of their sleep. It follows a tried and tested formula and my disciples are more than capable of replying to them on my behalf.

"The recipients are blissfully unaware it is not me personally responding to them. Nevertheless, if they choose to follow the advice given them, practice the exercises, and undertake the meditations, rather than just read the words, then they will discover something. Nevertheless, they continue writing to me. I cannot reply to them all and now I don't bother at all - I leave it to the disciples."

The Guru looked at the Visitor and held him within his glance. The Visitor felt uncomfortable and was not sure what was expected of him in this situation. After a little thought he decided to ask the old man a question.

"Did you actually have an intimate relationship with the Aunt?" Asked the Visitor. "The secretary seemed to think it highly unlikely."

The Guru looked at him and growled.

"Yet again your questioning is imprecise - you are not literal enough in your thought process and there is no real feeling or intention behind what you are seeking to know. All relationships are intimate. The degree of intimacy depends on how much each party is prepared to reveal to each other. The act of revelation determines the level of intimacy. This is of course not the answer you are looking for. I can only explain anything up to the level of our own intimacy. Come, let us work together."

The Visitor could not help but find the old man rather unpleasant and objectionable. Yet at the same time, however harsh the old man seemed to be, he could taste the absolute truth behind his words.

This was not what he had been expecting. He had always been under the impression an ashram would be a place of peace, harmony and love. He was confused. He picked up a hoe, and following the old man's example, started working up and down the rows of vegetables, removing the weeds and placing them in the wheelbarrow.

They worked together for an hour and a half in complete silence. The Visitor found the gentle exertion exhilarating.

Slowly he discovers an affinity with the hoe, the movement of his body and his breathing. It is a feeling similar to the one he experiences when working on one of his drawings. Then suddenly a warm sensation of energy courses through his spine, his arms, his legs - he can feel the whole of himself together at one moment with the surroundings. A sense of peace suffuses his being, generated, it appears, from within and without of himself. He pauses for a moment, looks up and sees the old man leaning on his hoe considering him carefully.

"So you see love and peace flow naturally in this place if you know how to follow the line. Do not try to analyse your feelings with your ordinary mind or you will lose what truly is. Now, for the moment we are finished here. Go to your room, wash and change for we need to go to the temple, just you and me. Time is in short supply, and we have much to discuss. Meet me in the temple in forty-five minutes."

Exactly forty-five minutes later the Visitor walked through the garden paths down toward the temple.

Much has been written of the beautiful temple situated beside this particular Ashram adjacent to the Holy River - the ornate pillars, the intricately carved archways of white marble, the brightly painted ceiling, and the alcoves housing the revered deities of the Hindu pantheon. The Visitor had read a great deal of this literature, yet nothing prepared him for the holy and tranquil calm emanating from the building.

He walked slowly through the open doorway and saw it for the first time in situ - the symbol which had been appropriated by his parents; the symbol which had become his company's logo; the symbol which formed the map of his company's 'Symbolic Psychometric Personality Assessment™'

It hung from the ceiling against the wall opposite the entrance - a cross of black granite inlayed with the leaves of a vine resting on a piece of golden marble shaped in the form of a six-pointed star partially enclosed within a circle of white marble. He stood transfixed by the sight of this object before noticing the old man sat cross legged on a cushion in the centre of temple floor opposite the symbol. There was a cushion placed next to him on his left-hand side. The Visitor knew instinctively he was meant to sit beside him.

He walks quietly from the doorway entrance and takes his place next to the Guru. As he does so he feels a spasm of anxiety course through his body. His head spins for a moment as he recognises the sensation of apprehension. He had always considered himself to be a person who did not needlessly concern himself over what others thought of him. Now, feeling the true power of a person with presence he feels insignificant and overawed - a young child, who regardless of what he previously believed about himself has in actuality barely scratched the surface of real knowledge.

He perceives the truth of the old man's intensity, his wisdom, his compassion and love. He can see the truth bubbling energetically in bright colours from the Guru's being - the old man had attained a level of being far greater than anything the Visitor has ever experienced.

They sit in silence for a several minutes before the Guru speaks.

"I am pleased you are feeling uncomfortable. Your life so far has been too easy. You suffer the illusion of being in control of your life - this has made you lazy. You play the observer in all you do without truly engaging. You rely on your art to provide you with an illusory sense of feeling. It is now time for you to place one foot in front of the other and start walking the line of your path. You have been dawdling and fritting along its edges for far too long - it is time to move. Tell me what do you see?"

The Visitor is silent for a moment. "Obviously I was expecting to see the sign hanging here, but what stands out is the vine growing from the centre and moving around the line of the cross. Although I inherited a version of the sign from my parents it is the vine which has been the formative motif of my life, though I have never really understood why."

He stops speaking and becomes thoughtful. He sits quietly awaiting a response from the Guru. When the reply is finally given the voice of the Guru seems to penetrate the whole of his being.

"Although it lies within the heart of the cross the Vine is of a much older provenance - it is not archetypal in the way of being. It reveals the power of intoxication, illusion, delusion, and truth. It lies beyond the reasoning of the rational mind (assuming there is such a thing), and a theoretical discussion on this subject would be a waste of the very short time we have together.

"Nevertheless, I will try to explain a little regarding the perception of its essence. It can only be known and felt through feeling - the taste is unique and yet the quality is forever changing - this is a personal challenge for you - to consider the symbol together with the vine and determine your truth. We are all part of the Vine - in some ways it could be said we are the Vine. All life on earth, every atom and molecule of the planet, are held together by the Vine. Simultaneously we are one within the Vine and yet each connection is truly unique in making up the whole. The life force of the Vine is love, but a love beyond the comprehension of most mortal beings. Your own personal connection with the Vine is what sets you out as a truth-sayer.

"The symbol was always meant to be dynamic. What was wrong in the development of your psychological tool was your interpretation was static, you failed to comprehend the fluidity of movement through all the spheres of our existence on a spiritual dimension. You also failed to register the vine in your deliberations. Consider the sign in its individual parts, and as a whole. Maybe you will find a truth. The only clue I can give you is that the sign is a map onto which humanity, if they so choose, may determine the journey of their return to the source of all being - it reveals the line of travel through the Vine toward the Divine Source of its own creation.

"You surely must realise there is only one purpose for a religion and only one truth. In their essence all genuine spiritual traditions follow the same trajectory - to return to the Divine Source of all existence. Naturally most traditions see their path as truly unique and different depending on the period of their inception. And most followers get lost trying to 'proselytise' their fundamental belief onto others. Many will cross the line and lose the way - this is the Divine will. Yet all and everything will be given the opportunity to return to the Source, though some will take longer to arrive home than others.

"Until you return to the Truth all 'truth' is different depending on the unique existence of each individual and the particular thread of their line. When a person tries to convince you to follow their way - to join them on their own path, they are living a lie. The honest teacher describes a path and reveals to you your own. The liar merely tries to justify their own non-existent way of living.

"As I explained in the garden many who feel a call to return seek an easy way towards enlightenment and there are many pseudo spiritual traditions who will provide them with an easing balm of pastimes to play at while they await the death of their mortal body. Your parents established one such tradition and it eventually evolved into the company you are chairman of. Such people, as indeed your parents were, will generally roam around from one tradition to another wandering aimlessly across the line of their life. I do not believe you have inherited their tendency. Your path has led you here for a very specific purpose - discover the intention and make of it what you can.

"No-one understands why I have allowed the Ashram to go to rack and ruin. They do not understand the need for the cyclical renewal of our way - nothing can remain static. This particular earthly life of mine is drawing to its inevitable closure and along with it my own Work in this dimension. Everything here will cease momentarily and move into a transitional phase during which a new guru will arise and the Ashram will be renewed.

"I am more than aware of the criticism floating in the minds of the people surrounding me. However, it is only I who can truly comprehend who I really am and what I have achieved in this life. My purpose for the moment is fulfilled.

"One day you may also be able to determine your purpose but only when you attain and maintain the degree of feeling this requires. A new phase of work is required in your life in order to achieve this - your ordinary way of being no longer satisfies you, and your business no longer needs you. Look around - everything decays and passes away.

"I am dying and will soon leave - stay with me until then. A new way for the ashram will arise and for a while, for a few, it will become a 'truth'. You are part of the transition - do not let your life finish before you have experienced it. You need to become aware of the chiming of the bell. This is all I have to say to you - there is nothing more I can offer you. It is for you to understand."

Silence pervades the temple. The Visitor remains sitting deep in a thoughtful meditation trying to allow what has been said to permeate his consciousness. The Guru stands up slowly and carefully walks toward the open door and away from the temple.

The Guru was not present at the evening meal - he informed the secretary he would eat alone. The disciples were to eat their meal in silence and then go into the meditation hall for Kirtan led by another of the elder residents. It was quite late in the evening when the Visitor finally returned to his bedroom. He lay down on the small bed and fell asleep immediately.

He awoke to the sound of a person knocking persistently at his door. It was still dark so he turned onto his stomach and reached across to turn on his bedside lamp. He swung himself upright and moved his legs onto the wooden floor, stood up, walked over to the door and opened it gently. The secretary was standing two and a half paces from the door. He brought his hands together and bowed towards the visitor with a quiet and gentle Namaste.

"I am sorry to bother you. Please could you join us in the master's lodgings. Our beloved Guruji has died within his sleep. The room attendant heard him calling out to your Aunt Miriam. He entered the room immediately and found the Guruji dead with an ecstatic smile on his face clutching the urn of your Aunt in both hands. It is now our duty to sit with him until dawn to help with the returning of his soul to the source of his belief."

The Visitor picked up his watch from the bedside table to check the time. He stared at it for a moment before he realised the second hand was not moving - the watch had stopped at exactly 4.00am.

"What time is it?" He enquired.

"It is 4.25am - our Guruji died approximately twenty-five minutes ago. He has left a letter for you. He gave it to me a week before you arrived with strict instructions only to hand it over to you if anything happened to him."

The secretary passed over a sealed envelope, turned away and stepped slowly down the fourteen steps through the open archway into the garden. The Visitor watched the secretary leave and looked out over the balcony to observe him walk over to the master's lodgings. He pauses for a moment holding the letter in his hand before moving over to his bed where he sits down and opens it. The letter was written by hand in a lavender coloured ink in a traditional style of calligraphy - he is immediately taken by the quality of draughtsmanship.

Dear William

I am writing this letter to you before we have even met in the flesh. Do not be surprised - I have been aware of you for some time. I have awaited your coming with a degree of trepidation, yet also with hopeful anticipation - for your arrival will mark the timing of my death. I have heard the sounding chime of the bell. There is no doubt you are a truth-sayer. I hope I will have had the time to lead you in the right direction of your personal line. If I have I ask you to treat my followers with love and respect. The mantle of truth-sayer is both a personal blessing and a curse. You cannot hide from the role - it was chosen for you by a much higher power. What you do with your future, however, is up to you, yet I hope you will choose to stay with us for a while.

So, a gift I will leave you. I have named you as my chief mourner - a symbolic gesture of course and a duty you will have no understanding of as you read these words. Do not worry overmuch. I am sure you will find the ritual of Antyesti suitably uncomfortable - most westerners do. The cremation will occur within 24 hours of my death which will give the secretary plenty of time to explain the importance of your duties. There is to be only one break with tradition - I demand the urn containing the ashes of Miriam to be cremated with me. We will enter the Holy River together.

Finally, I offer you my deepest blessings. May the Truth be your guiding principle.

Swami Satsangi

The cremation was held in the evening of the day in which he died. As William watched the flames of the pyre slowly die down something stirred inside and outside of him - a deep sensation of compassionate love. He had never sensed a power like it before in the summation of his life so far. Instinctively he knew that for a moment he was experiencing the Source of everything. There was no William - he existed and yet he did not exist. He was in tune with the Vine, he could feel it and was within it, he could observe it in all its totality - each and every path together with the direction of their movement in eternity.

It lasted only for the shortest of a moment of time. He became William once more, but no longer quite the same William. A movement had occurred within him revealing the direction of his path together with the realisation he was about to take his first steps consciously along its line.

He had undertaken his duties as Chief Mourner respectfully. In reality the majority of the essential rituals were undertaken by the secretary. Nevertheless, he had circumambulated around the pyre, thrown the water pot and lit the flames. The Kapala Krya was undertaken by the secretary - he did not feel he had the requisite capability to pierce through the burning skull with the bamboo stave.

William walked slowly back up from the temple and took a shower. He changed his clothes and walked down to the refectory where he sat down at the end table in the seat next to the one which would have been taken by Guruji. He placed both feet on the floor and his hands palm up on his upper legs with fingers touching the thumbs. He found sensation and opened his eyes. One by one the members of the community walked thoughtfully through the door and took their places at the table. The Secretary sat opposite him.

"Our Guruji told us before you came here you were also Satsangi - the seeker of truth. William, may we ask you a question - what is Truth?"

William contemplated the question for a while realising that if he answered his life would change beyond anything he had previously imagined for himself. He tasted the Truth - golden, silver, milk white and olive black. He felt the energy as each colour resounded and radiated their essence within his entire being. He experienced the fruit of Eden. His path from now on would be a way of knowledge, creativity, love and service, as he himself followed the line towards the source of his life. He looked up at the secretary and held him in his eyes.

"The seed of truth is contained within the line of each individual's path as revealed through the Vine. The seed germinates and grows to its fruition as you move in the direction of being. It conceals itself if you move away from the line of its apparent direction. If you stop still the seed of truth stagnates and its essence of love is lost - it becomes the lie. If you move backwards the temptations of identification will overwhelm you and you will become the lie itself - the seed of truth will become diseased. You can only perceive the level of truth unto the level of your own being. Here your journey has become stagnant - you failed to follow the path your Guru revealed to you. Now you must find it again and follow it willingly in love, together as the seekers of truth. In this way the seed will once again renew itself."

"Satsangi William, will you stay with us and help us through our transition? Will you teach truth to us?"

William looks up and behind the head of the secretary, on the far end wall, he sees for the first time, painted on it, the Symbol. It is exactly as the girls had created it for the Aunt. There was the black cross, bearing an intricate vine traced within it, resting on a golden six-pointed star, partially enclosed within circle. The top of the circle is coloured in gold which merges into silver, then into a creamy white, and finally into black.

He looks closely at the centre of the cross. Again he notices the small circle in the centre. As he looks it appears to grow larger - moving from two dimensions into the third transforming itself into a perfectly round sphere. As he studies the sphere it transforms again into a multi-faceted emerald cut diamond sparkling in a non-existent sun, before returning to being a small, relatively insignificant circle in the centre of the cross. He looks again but the symbol has vanished from the wall. It has returned to how he remembered it being, a plain wall painted in a dingy off-white brown.

William considered his answer and when he spoke it was with the quiet calm confidence of the truth-sayer.

"A teacher may reveal your path. A teacher may show you how to follow the line of the path. A teacher may help you to reach the doorway of Truth. However, the teacher cannot open the door for you, for only you can achieve this. And your ability to do so resides in your relationship with the Divine. Only within this most secret and personal relationship is the door opened and only when it is opened, and you still hear the chiming of the bell, will the fullness of Truth be revealed to you."

Conclusion

'There is a question frequently revealed in the heart of humanity - why am I here?
Beware the question for it may not hold the answer you are looking for.'

And as we move toward the end of our tales you may well be asking what right we have to discuss the question of Truth when we are merely the summation and collective conscious of existence up to the point of death - for unless the finality of the mortal body beyond expiration is brought into the equation surely there can be no answer. Of course you may well consider there is no question to be answered.

If there is no question to answer there is no truth to be revealed unto you, and, if you hold no question you may surely count yourself as one of the blessed.

Yes, you will live in solitary pain but you will never find the cause. You will develop the ability to lay the blame for all your negative experiences in life on the others surrounding you - your parents, your siblings, your children, your friends and acquaintances, the government of your societies, et al. - you will feel comforted and vindicated by the simple lie that none of it is your fault - you are not responsible, everyone else is.

Many people believe in nothing and are barely aware of their own life on earth coming to its inevitable conclusion - they choose to remain permanently in sleep.

Nevertheless, If you hold the living question then quite possibly you may feel cursed.

You will live in the pain of your search for the answer. You will come to realise it is only you who are responsible for what you feel. Maybe you will long for the luxurious sleep of those who surround you. Maybe you will endeavour to join them.

What we can affirm, without the merest shadow of a doubt, is that the majority of people within humanity who find a degree of satisfaction in their life are generally those who are in possession of a question providing them with both purpose and meaning whilst they seek its answer.

But be aware, a question loses its power as soon as it has been answered.

Do you have a question? If so feel free to ask.

In the meantime let us bring an end to our tales once and for all.

Chapter 10 - The Child

'In the arrogance of our knowing we remain
unaware of who we are.'

At the conclusion of any story there is an ending. In this particular narrative it ends with the Child who had already grown up before realising he was still a child...

His wife turns around to him. "You really should accept the job my brother has offered you."

Acknowledgements

'Within the Divine grace of Love
May we all live in the truth of who
and what we can become.
So Be It'

The Insidious Line is the final part of the Insidious Vine trilogy. It concludes a long journey undertaken over ten years – it has been a blessing and I have been fortunate to receive the support of many people along the way.

I have purposedly described the series as esoteric with a dystopian orientation and it is probably helpful if I define exactly what I mean. The term esoteric is often misunderstood and frequently described as relating to some hidden teaching only available to a selected few and transmitted orally from teacher to pupil.

From my perspective I would define esoteric not as a hidden teaching but an inner teaching for the development of self, as opposed to the exoteric which is concerned with outer life and social norms. It is not hidden at all and whilst it is generally transmitted orally it is readily available and accessible to anyone prepared to consider and observe there inner life as it relates to the universe surrounding us.

There are many teachers, though they will generally not be found in the streets and fairs hawking their wares. In reality the more you proceed on the path toward inner conscious awareness the more you realise that every single person you meet and engage with (indeed every single character in these stories) is a teacher.

So finally I would like to acknowledge all my teachers – thank you for your love, compassion, support, and instruction.

About Paul Ogden

Paul is a writer, musician, and composer with a keen interest in psychology and philosophy. He is also a business and voice coach specialising in the way people interact with each other from day to day. He is a practitioner of Conscious Body Awareness - a form of 'mindfulness' - which forms the basis of his work with others and features within his writing. He is influenced by the 'Work' of G.I. Gurdjiefff and the 'Method' of Dr Moshe Feldenkrais.

The first book in the series (The Insidious Vine)is available in a variety of formats as an audio album with a complete music score - see www.theinsidiousvine.com for more details. For more information or if you have any questions about the trilogy contact Paul by email

Non-fiction books by Paul

The Feldenkrais Method for Executive Coaches, Managers, and Business Leaders (Moving in All Directions): Co-written with Garet Newell, with a foreword by Sue Knight. Routledge Focus – ISBN 978-1-138-23091-0

www.ingramcontent.com/pod-product-compliance
Lightning Source LLC
Chambersburg PA
CBHW030119260626
47156CB00008B/2719